KU-431-225

The stirring story of the life and times of Richard Bolitho is told in Alexander Kent's bestselling novels, all available in Arrow.

Also in Arrow by Alexander Kent

ALEXANDER KENT

*Midshipman Bolitho
and the 'Avenger'*

ARROW BOOKS

Arrow Books Limited
17–21 Conway Street, London w1p 6jd

An imprint of the Hutchinson Publishing Group

London Melbourne Sydney Auckland
Johannesburg and agencies
throughout the world

First published by Hutchinson 1978
Arrow edition 1979
Reprinted 1983
© Bolitho Maritime Productions Ltd 1978

Made and printed in Great Britain
by The Anchor Press Ltd
Tiptree, Essex

ISBN 0 09 919880 0

To All Midshipmen
Past and Present

Contents

I

Home From the Sea

With an impressive clatter of wheels the stage-coach shivered to a halt beside the inn's courtyard and its handful of weary passengers gave a sigh of relief. It was early December, the year 1773, and Falmouth, like most of Cornwall, was covered in a blanket of snow and slush. Standing in the dull afternoon light, with its four horses steaming from their hard drive, the coach seemed to have no colour, as it was coated with mud from axles to roof.

Midshipman Richard Bolitho jumped down and stood for a few moments just staring at the old, familiar inn and the weathered buildings beyond. It had been a painful ride. Only fifty-five miles from Plymouth to here, but it had taken two days. The coach had gone inland, almost into Bodmin Moor, to avoid flooding from the River Fowey, and the coachman had firmly refused to move at night because of the treacherous roads. Bolitho suspected he was more afraid of highwaymen than weather. Those *gentlemen* found it much easier to prey on coaches bogged down on muddy, rutted tracks than to match shots with an eagle-eyed guard on the King's highway.

He forgot the journey, the bustling ostlers who were releasing the horses from their harness, also the other passengers as they hurried toward the inn's inviting warmth, and favoured the moment.

It had been a year and two months since he had left Falmouth to join the seventy-four-gun ship of the line *Gorgon* at Spithead. Now she lay at Plymouth for a much-needed refit and overhaul, and he, Richard Bolitho, had come home for a well-earned leave.

Bolitho held out his hand to steady his travelling companion as he climbed down to join him in the bitter wind. Midshipman Martyn Dancer had joined *Gorgon* on the same day as himself, and like Bolitho was seventeen years old.

'Well, Martyn, we have *arrived*.'

Bolitho smiled, glad Dancer had come with him. His home was in London, and quite different in a thousand ways from his own. Whereas the Bolithos had been sea officers for generations, Dancer's father was a rich City of London tea merchant. But if their worlds were miles apart, Bolitho felt towards Martyn Dancer as he would to a brother.

When *Gorgon* had anchored, and the mail had been brought aboard, Dancer had discovered that his parents were abroad. He had immediately suggested that Bolitho should keep him company in London, but *Gorgon*'s first lieutenant, the ever-watchful Mr Verling, had said icily, 'I should think not indeed.

Alone in *that* city, your father would see me damned for it!'

So Dancer had readily accepted Bolitho's invitation. Bolitho was secretly glad. And he was eager to see his family again, for them to see him, and the change that fourteen months of hard service had offered him. Like his friend, he was leaner, if that were possible, more confident, and above all grateful to have survived both storm and shot.

The coach guard touched his hat and took the coins which Bolitho thrust into his gloved fist.

'Don't 'ee fear, zur. I'll tell the innkeeper to send your chests up to the house directly.' He jerked his thumb at the inn windows, already glowing with lantern light. 'Now I'll join me fellow travellers for an hour, then on to Penzance.' He walked away, adding, 'Good luck to 'ee, young gennlemen.'

Bolitho watched him thoughtfully. So many Bolithos had mounted or dismounted from coaches here. On their way to far-off places, returning from one ship or another. Some never came back at all.

He threw his blue boat-cloak round his shoulders and said, 'We'll walk. Get the blood alive again, eh?'

Dancer nodded, his teeth chattering uncontrollably. Like Bolitho, he was very tanned, and was still unable to accept the violent change of weather and climate after a year in and around the African coastline.

Now, as they strode through the mud and slush, past the old church and ancient trees, it was hard to believe it had ever happened. Searching for corsairs, retaking the brig *Sandpiper* and using her to destroy a pirate's ship after a chase through dangerous reefs. Men had died, many more had suffered from all the countless burdens which beset sailors everywhere. Bolitho had fought hand to hand, had been made to kill, had watched one of the *Gorgon*'s midshipmen fall dead during an attack on a slaver's stronghold. They were no longer boys. They had become young men together.

'There it is.' Bolitho pointed at the big grey house, square and uncompromising, almost the same colour as the low, scudding clouds and the headland beyond.

Through the gates and up to the broad doorway. He did not even have to reach for one of the massive iron-ringed handles, for the doors swung inwards and he saw Mrs Tremayne, the housekeeper, rushing to meet him, her red face beaming with pleasure.

She hugged him to her, overwhelming him, bringing back even more memories. Her smell of clean linen and lavender, of kitchens and hung bacon. She was well over sixty-five, and was as much a part of the house as its foundations.

She rocked him back and forth like a child, although he was a head taller than she.

'Oh, young Master Dick, what have they done to 'ee?' She was almost in tears. 'You'm as thin as a reed, nothin' to 'ee at all. I'll soon put some meat on your bones.'

She saw Dancer for the first time and released him reluctantly.

Bolitho grinned, embarrassed but pleased at her concern. She had been far worse when he had first gone to sea at the age of twelve.

'This is my friend, Martyn Dancer. He's to stay with us.'

They all turned as Bolitho's mother appeared on the great stairway.

'And you will be most welcome.'

Dancer watched her, entranced. He had heard plenty about Harriet Bolitho during the long sea-watches and the rare moments of peace between decks. But she was like no woman in his imaginary picture. She seemed too young to be Richard's mother, too fragile even to be left so often alone in this great stone house below the Pendennis Castle headland.

'Mother.'

Bolitho went to her and they embraced for a long moment. And still Dancer watched. Richard, his friend, whom he had come to know so well, usually so good at hiding his feelings behind an impassive face and those calm grey eyes. Whose hair was as black as his own was fair, who could show emotion at the death of a friend, but who had become a lion in battle, looked more like her suitor than a son.

She said to Dancer, 'How long?'

It was calmly put, but he sensed the edge in her question.

Bolitho replied for him. 'Four weeks. Maybe longer if. . . .'

She reached up and touched his hair.

'I know, Dick. That word *if*. The Navy must have invented it.'

She put her hands through their arms and linked them together.

'But you will be home for Christmas. And you have a friend. That is good. Your father is still away in India.' She sighed. 'And I am afraid Felicity is married and with her husband's regiment in Canterbury.'

Bolitho turned and studied her gravely. He had been thinking only of himself. Of his homecoming, his own pride at what he had done. And she had been made to face everything alone, as was too often the case with the women who married into the Bolitho family.

His sister, Felicity, who was now nineteen, had been very happy to receive one of the young officers from the local garrison. While he was away she had married him, and had gone.

Bolitho had guessed that his only brother, Hugh, would be away. He was four years his senior, the apple of his father's eye, and at present a lieutenant aboard a frigate.

He asked awkwardly, 'And Nancy? Is she well, Mother?'

Her face lit up, making her appear her old self again.

'Indeed she is, Dick, although she is out visiting, despite the weather.'

Dancer felt strangely relieved. He had heard a good deal about Nancy, the youngest of the family. She would be about sixteen, and something of a beauty, if her mother was anything to judge by.

Bolitho saw his friend's expression and said, 'That is good news.'

She looked from one to the other and laughed. 'I see your point.'

'I'll take Martyn to his room, Mother.'

She nodded, watching them as they climbed the stairway, past the watching portraits of long-dead Bolithos.

'When the post-boy told us that the *Gorgon* was in Plymouth, I knew you would come home, Dick. I'd never forgive your Captain Conway if he'd denied me that pleasure!'

Bolitho thought of the captain, aloof, impressively calm no matter what the hazards. He had never really pictured him as a ladies' man.

Dancer was studying one portrait at the turn of the stairway.

Bolitho said quietly, 'My grandfather Denziel. He was with Wolfe at Quebec. Grand old man, I think. Sometimes I can't remember if I really knew him, or if it was what my father told me about him which remains.'

Dancer grinned. 'He looks a lively sort. And Rear Admiral, no less!'

He followed Bolitho along the landing, hearing the wind and sleet against the windows. It felt strange after a ship's constant movement, the sounds and smells of a crowded man-of-war.

It was always the same with midshipmen. They were constantly hungry, and being chased and harried in every direction. Now, if only for a few days, he would find peace, and if Mrs Tremayne had anything to do with it, a full stomach too.

Bolitho opened a door for him. 'One of the maids will bring your things, Martyn.' He faltered, his eyes like the sea beyond the headland. 'I'm glad you came. Once or twice,' he hesitated, ' . . . back over the months, I thought I would never be coming here again. Having you with me makes it feel complete.'

He swung away, and Dancer closed the door quietly behind him.

Dancer knew exactly what he had meant, and was moved to have shared the moment with him.

He crossed to a window and peered through the streaming glass. Almost lost in the winter's gloom the sea was lively and criss-crossed with angry crests.

It was out there waiting for them to return.

He smiled and started to undress.

Well, it could damned well wait a bit longer!

'So, Martyn, what did you think of your first free evening?'

The two midshipmen sat on either side of a roaring log fire, legs outstretched, eyes drooping from the heat and the biggest meal Mrs Tremayne had prepared for some time.

Dancer raised his goblet and watched the flames change colour through the ruby port and smiled contentedly.

'Something akin to a miracle.'

It had been a lengthy meal, with Bolitho's mother and his young sister Nancy both eager and willing just to let them talk. Bolitho had found himself wondering how many tales had been passed across that same table, some embroidered no doubt, but all true.

Nancy had worn a new gown for the occasion, which she apparently had made in Truro. '*The latest thing in France.*' It had been low-cut, and although her mother had frowned once or twice, it made her look younger rather than wanton.

She was much more like her mother than her sister, who took after the Bolitho side of the family, with the same ready smile which had charmed Captain James Bolitho when he had taken a Scottish girl for his wife.

Nancy had made a great impression on Dancer, and Bolitho guessed it was probably mutual.

Outside the curtained windows it was quieter, the sleet having given way to snow, which had already covered the outbuildings and stables in a thick, glistening blanket. No one would be moving very far tonight, Bolitho thought, and he pitied the coach on its way to Penzance.

How still the house seemed, the servants having gone to bed long since, leaving the two friends to drowse or yarn as so inclined.

'Tomorrow we'll go to the harbour, Martyn, although Mr Tremayne tells me there's little anchored in the Roads at present worth looking at.'

The male half of the Tremayne family was the household steward and general handyman. Like the other retainers he was old. Although the Seven Years War had ended ten years back, it had left a lot of unfilled gaps in the villages and hamlets. Some young men had fallen in battle, others had liked the outside world better than their own rural communities and had stayed away. In Falmouth you were usually a sailor or a farm worker, and that was how it had always been.

'Maybe it will be clear enough for us to ride, eh?' Bolitho smiled. '*Ride?*'

'We don't go everywhere in London by coach, you know!'

Their laughter stopped in mid-air as two loud bangs echoed from the front doorway.

'Who is abroad at this hour?' Dancer was already on his feet.

Bolitho held up his hand. 'Wait.' He strode to a cupboard and took out a pistol. 'It is well to be careful, even here.'

Together they opened the big double doors, feeling the cold wind wrap around their overheated bodies like a shroud.

Bolitho saw it was his father's gamekeeper, John Pendrith, who had a cottage close to the house. He was a powerfully built, morose sort of man, who was much feared by the local poachers. And there were quite a few of them.

'Oi be sorry to disturb you, zur.' He gestured vaguely with his long-barrelled musket. 'But one o' the lads come up from the town. Old Reverend Walmsley said it were the best thing to do.'

'Come in, John.'

Bolitho closed the doors after them. The big gamekeeper's presence, let alone his air of mystery, had made him uneasy in some way.

Pendrith took a glass of brandy and warmed himself by the fire, the steam rising from his thick coat like a cart-horse.

Whatever it was, it must be important for old Walmsley, the rector, to send a messenger here.

'This lad found a corpse, zur. Down on the fore-shore. Bin in the water for some while, 'e reckons.' He looked up, his eyes bleak. 'It were Tom Morgan, zur.'

Bolitho bit his lip. 'The revenue officer?'

'Aye. 'E'd bin done in afore 'e went into the water, so the lad says.'

There were sounds on the stairway, and then Bolitho's mother, wrapped in a green velvet cloak, hurried down towards them, her eyes questioning.

Bolitho said, 'I can deal with it, Mother. They've found Tom Morgan on the foreshore.'

'Dead?'

Pendrith said bluntly, 'Murdered, ma'am.' To Bolitho he explained, 'Y'see, zur, with the soldiers away, an' the squire in Bath, the old Reverend turned to you like.' He grimaced. 'You bein' a King's officer, so to speak.'

Dancer exclaimed, 'Surely there's somebody else?'

Bolitho's mother was already pulling at the bell-rope, her face pale but determined.

'No. They always come to the house. I'll tell Corker to saddle two horses. You go with them, John.'

Bolitho said quietly, 'I'd rather he was here, with you.' He squeezed her arm. 'It's all right. Really. I'm not the boy who went off to sea with an apple in his pocket. Not any more.'

It was strange how easily it came to him. One minute he had been ready for bed. Now he was alert, every nerve keen to sudden danger. From the look on Dancer's face, he knew he was equally affected.

Pendrith said, 'I sent the lad back to watch over

the body. You'll remember the place, zur. The cove where you an' your brother overturned that dory an' took a good beatin' for it!' He gave a slow grin.

One of the maids appeared, and listened to her instructions before hurrying away to tell Corker, the coachman, what to do.

Bolitho said, 'No time to change into uniform, Martyn. We'll go as we are.'

Both he and his friend were dressed in mixed clothing which they had borrowed from chests and cupboards throughout the house. In a house which was, and had always been, a home for sea officers, there was naturally a plentiful supply of spare coats and breeches.

They were ready to leave in fifteen minutes. From drowsy relaxation to crisp preparedness. If the Navy had given them nothing else, it had taught them that. The only way to stay alive in a ship-of-war was to stay vigilant.

Horses clattered on the stones outside the doors, and Bolitho asked, 'Who is the lad who found the body, John?'

Pendrith shrugged. 'The smith's son.' He made a motion with his finger to his forehead. 'Not all there. Moonstruck.'

Bolitho kissed his mother on the cheek. Her skin was like ice.

'Go to bed. I'll be back soon. Tomorrow we'll send someone to the magistrate in Truro, or to the dragoons.'

They were out and mounted before the swirling snow made their journey more difficult.

There were few lights to be seen in the town, and Bolitho guessed that most sensible folk were in bed.

Dancer called, 'I suppose you know most people hereabouts, or they know you? That's the difference 'twixt here and London!'

Bolitho tucked his chin into his collar and urged the horse through the snow. Fancy Pendrith remembering about the dory. He and his brother had been competing with each other. Hugh had been a midshipman then, while he had been waiting the chance to join his first ship. Their father had been beside himself with anger, which was unusual. Not for what they had done, but because of the worry they had given their mother. It was true too that he had beaten them both to make them remember it.

Soon they heard the sea, rumbling and hissing against the headland and the necklace of rocks below. It was eerie under this mantle of snow. Strange shapes loomed through the darkness, while trees shed great pieces of their white burden to make sounds like a footpad running through the night.

It took all of an hour to discover the cove, which was little more than a cleft in the solid rock with a small, sloping beach. The smith's son waited for them with a lantern, humming to himself and stamping his feet on the wet sand for comfort.

Bolitho dismounted and said, 'Hold my horse, Martyn.' The animal was nervous and restless, as horses often were in the presence of death.

The corpse lay on its back, arms outflung, mouth open.

Bolitho forced himself to kneel beside the dead revenue man.

'Was he like this, Tim?'

'Aye, zur.' The youth giggled. 'I was a-lookin' for. . . .' He shrugged. 'Anythin'.'

Bolitho knew all about the local blacksmith. His wife had left him long ago, and he sent his weak-minded son out of his cottage whenever he was entertaining one of his many female visitors. It was said that he had caused the boy's mind to go by hitting him as a baby in a fit of rage.

The youth said as an afterthought, ' 'Is pockets is empty, zur. Nary a coin.'

Dancer called, 'Is it the man, Dick?'

Bolitho stood up. 'Aye. His throat's been cut.'

The Cornish coast was renowned for its smugglers. But the revenue men were seldom injured in their efforts to find and catch them. With the squire away, and without his additional support as local magistrate, it would mean sending for aid from Truro or elsewhere.

He recalled the gamekeeper's words and said to Dancer, 'Well, my friend, it seems we are not free of our duty after all.'

Dancer soothed the restless horses. 'I thought it too good to last.'

Bolitho said to the youth, 'Go to the inn and tell the landlord to rouse some men. We'll need a hand-cart.' He waited for his words to sink in. 'Can you manage that?'

He nodded jerkily. 'Oi think so, zur.' He scratched his head. 'Oi bin 'ere a long time.'

Dancer reached down and handed him some money. 'That's for all your trouble, er, Tim.'

As the youth stumbled away, chattering to himself, Bolitho shouted after him, 'And don't give it to your father!'

Then he said, 'Better tether the horses and give me a hand. The tide's on the make and we'll lose the body in a half-hour otherwise.'

They pulled the sodden corpse up the shelving beach, and Bolitho thought of other men he had seen die, yelling and cursing in the heat and din of battle. That had been terrible. But to die like this man, alone and terrified, and then to be thrown in the sea like some discarded rubbish seemed far worse.

By the time help arrived and the corpse was taken to the church, and then they had all gone to the inn to sustain themselves, it was almost dawn.

The horses made little noise as they returned to the house, but Bolitho knew his mother would hear and be waiting.

As she hurried to greet them he said firmly, 'No, Mother. You must go back to bed.'

She looked at him strangely and then smiled. 'It is *good* to have a man in the house once again.'

2

The 'Avenger'

Bolitho and Dancer entered the front door, stamping their boots free of mud and snow, their faces and limbs tingling from a brisk ride across the headland.

It had all but stopped snowing, and here and there gorse or shrub were poking through, like stuffing from a torn mattress.

Bolitho said quietly, 'We have company, Martyn.'

He had already seen the coach in the yard where Corker and his assistant were tending to a fine pair of horses. He had recognized the crest on the coach door, that of Sir Henry Vyvyan, whose sprawling estates lay some ten miles to the west of Falmouth. A rich and powerful man, and one of the country's most respected magistrates as well.

He was standing by the crackling fire, watching Mrs Tremayne as she put the finishing touches to a tankard of mulled wine. She had her own receipt for it, with carefully measured ingredients of sugar, spice and beaten egg yolk.

Vyvyan was an impressive figure, and when

Bolitho had been much younger he had been more than a little frightened of the man. Tall, broad-shouldered, with a large hooked nose, his countenance was dominated by a black patch over his left eye. From above his nose, diagonally across the eye socket and deep into the cheek bone was a terrible scar. Whatever had done it must have clawed out the eye like a hook.

The remaining eye fixed on the two midshipmen, and Vyvyan said loudly, 'Glad to see you, young Richard, an' your friend.' He glanced at Bolitho's mother who was sitting by the far window. 'You must be right proud, ma'am.'

Bolitho knew that Vyvyan rarely spent his time on useless visits. He was something of a mystery, although his swift justice against footpads and highwaymen on and around his estates was well known and generally respected. He was said to have made his fortune privateering against the French and along the Spanish Main. Others hinted at slavery and the rum trade. They were all probably wrong, Bolitho thought.

It was strange how unreal the revenue man's death had seemed as they had ridden hard along the rutted coast road. It had been two nights since they had stood by the corpse with the smith's moonstruck son, and now with a bright sky to drive the shadows away from the snow and the hillsides, it had all become like part of a bad dream.

Vyvyan was saying in his deep voice, 'So I says to meself, ma'am, with Squire Roxby an' his family enjoyin' themselves in Bath, an' the military away

disportin' themselves like dandies at our purses'
expense, who better than meself to get over to
Falmouth an' take the strain? I see it as me duty,
especially as poor Tom Morgan was a tenant of
mine. He lived just outside Helston, a stout, reliable
yeoman. He'll be sorely missed, not least by his family,
I'm thinkin'.'

Bolitho watched his mother, seeing her hands
gripping the arms of her chair, the relief on her even
features. She was glad Sir Henry had come. To res-
tore security and kill the dangers of rumour. Bolitho
had heard plenty of that on their two days of leave.
Tales of smugglers, and spine-chilling talk of witchcraft near some of the smaller fishing villages. She
was also relieved that Vyvyan and not her youngest
son was to carry the responsibility.

Vyvyan took the steaming tankard from Mrs
Tremayne and said approvingly, 'God swamp me,
ma'am, if I didn't hold Mrs Bolitho as a dear friend
I'd lure you to Vyvyan Manor all for meself! There's
none in the whole county who can mull wine like you.'

Dancer cleared his throat. 'What do you intend,
sir?'

The solitary eye swivelled towards him and held
steady.

'All done, me boy.' He spoke cheerfully and offhandedly, like one who is used to making and following through decisions. 'Soon as I heard the news I
sent word to Plymouth. The port admiral is a friend.'
The eyelid dropped in a wink. 'And I'd heard that
your people have been active of late against the
smugglin' *gentry*.'

Bolitho pictured the big two-decker, *Gorgon*, laid up for repairs, her decks probably covered in snow. It would take longer than anticipated. Captain Conway might well see fit to grant extended leave to his junior officers. After all, when she put to sea again it could be several years before the *Gorgon* touched England once more.

Vyvyan added, 'The admiral will send a ship to deal with this matter. I'll have no murderin' scum working *my* coast!'

Bolitho remembered that some of Vyvyan's land ran down to the sea itself, from the dreaded Lizard to somewhere near the Manacles. A dangerous and cruel coastline. It would take a brave smuggler to try and land a catch there and face Vyvyan's rough justice at the end of it.

Bolitho turned as his mother said softly, 'I'm grateful for your trouble, Sir Henry.' She looked pale, more so in the reflected glare from the snow outside.

Vyvyan regarded her affectionately. 'But for that damned husband of yours, ma'am, I'd have set me cap at you, even if I am a cut-about old villain!'

She laughed. 'I'll tell him when he returns. It may make him quit the sea.'

Vyvyan downed the last of the wine and waved another ladle aside. 'No, I must be off now. Tell that fool of a coachman to get ready, if you please!' To the room at large he added, 'No, don't do that, ma'am. England will need all her sailors again afore long. Neither the Dons nor the French Court will rest until they have bared their metal against us for another attempt.' He laughed loudly. 'Well, let 'em!' He faced the two midshipmen. 'With lads like these, I think we can rest easy at night!'

With a hug for Mrs Bolitho and heavy slaps on the back for the midshipmen he stamped out into the hall, bellowing for his coachman.

Dancer grinned. 'His man must be deaf!'

Bolitho asked, 'Is it time to eat, Mother? We're starving!'

She smiled at them warmly. 'Soon now. Sir Henry's visit was unexpected.'

Two more days passed, each full of interest, and neither spoiling their escape from discipline and the routine life of shipboard.

Then the postboy, as he called at the house for something hot to drink, confided that a vessel had been sighted standing inshore towards the entrance to Carrick Roads.

The wind had veered considerably, and Bolitho knew it would take all of an hour for the incoming vessel to reach an anchorage.

He asked the postboy what she was, and he replied with a grimace, 'King's ship, sir. Cutter by the looks of 'er.'

A cutter. Probably one of those used by the Revenue Service, or better still, under naval command.

He said quickly, 'Shall we go and see her?'

Dancer was already looking for his coat. 'I'm ready.'

Bolitho's mother threw up her hands. 'No sooner back and you want to go looking at ships again! Just like your father!'

The air was keen-edged, like ice, but by the time they had walked through the town to the harbour they were glowing like stoves. Good food, with regular sleep and exercise, had worked wonders for both of them.

Together they stood on the jetty and watched the slow-moving vessel tacking towards her anchorage. She was some seventy feet in length, with a massive beam of over twenty. Single-masted, and with a rounded, blunt bow, she looked cumbersome and heavy, but Bolitho knew from what he had seen elsewhere that properly handled cutters could use their great sail area to tack within five points of the wind and in most weathers. She carried a vast, loose-footed mainsail, and also a squared topsail. A jib and fore completed her display of canvas, although Bolitho knew she could set more, even studding sails if required.

She was now turning lazily into the wind, her canvas vanishing deftly as her hands prepared to drop anchor. A red ensign and masthead pendant made the only colour against the pewter sky, and Bolitho felt the same old feeling he always did when seeing a part, even a small part, of his own world.

Blunt and clumsy she might appear, lacking the glinting broadsides and proud figureheads of larger men-of-war, she was nevertheless somebody's own command.

He saw the anchor splash down, the usual bustle at the tackles to sway the jolly boat up and over the bulwark.

Across the choppy water they both heard the

twitter of calls, and pictured the scene on board. In that seventy feet of hull they carried a company of nearly sixty souls, although how they managed to sleep, eat and work in such cramped space was hard to fathom. They shared the hull with anchor cables, water, provisions, powder and shot. It left few inches for comfort.

The jolly boat was in the water now, and Bolitho saw the gleam of white breeches beneath a blue coat as the vessel's commander climbed down to be pulled ashore.

As the tide and wind swung the cutter to her cable Bolitho saw her name painted across her raked quarter. *Avenger*. The dead revenue man would have approved, he thought grimly.

A small knot of onlookers had gathered on the wall to watch the newcomer. But not too many. People who lived by and off the sea were always wary of a King's ship, no matter how small.

Bolitho started as the boat hooked on to the jetty stairs and a burly seaman hurried towards him and knuckled his forehead.

'Mr Midshipman Bolitho, sir?'

Dancer chuckled. 'Even out of uniform you are recognized, Dick!'

The seaman added, 'My cap'n wishes a word, sir.'

Mystified, they walked to the stairs as the cocked hat and shoulders of *Avenger*'s commander appeared above the wet stones.

Bolitho stared with amazement. '*Hugh!*'

His brother regarded him impassively. 'Aye, Richard.' He nodded to Dancer, and then called to his coxswain, 'Return to the ship. My compliments to Mr Gloag, and tell him I will signal when I require the boat.'

Bolitho watched him, his feelings mixed and confused. Hugh was supposed to be in a frigate, or so he thought. He had changed quite a lot since their last meeting. The lines at his mouth and jaw were deeper, and his voice carried the rasp of authority. But the rest was unchanged. The black hair like his own, and like some of the portraits in the house, tied above his collar with a neat bow. Steady eyes, strained after long hours of sea duty, and the same old air of supreme confidence which had brought them to blows in the past.

They fell in step, Hugh thrusting past the onlookers with barely a glance.

As they walked he said, 'Is Mother well?' But he sounded distant, his mind elsewhere.

'She'll be glad to see you, Hugh. It will make it a real Christmas.'

Hugh glanced at Dancer. 'You've all been having a time for yourselves in the old *Gorgon*, I believe?'

Bolitho hid a smile. There it was again. The barb, the hint of disbelief.

Dancer nodded. 'You read of it, sir?'

'Some.' Hugh quickened his pace. 'Also I saw the admiral at Plymouth and spoke with your captain.' He stopped by the broad gateway, his eyes examining the house as if for the first time. 'I may as well tell you now. You have been placed under my orders until this local matter is cleared up, or my vacancies have been filled.'

Bolitho stared at him, angered by his abruptness, sorry for Dancer's position.

'Vacancies?'

Hugh regarded him calmly. 'Aye. I had to send my senior and some good hands aboard a prize last week. The Navy is hard put for spare officers and men, Richard, although you would not know about that, of course. It may be sunshine in Africa, but it is icy reality here!'

'Did you *ask* for us?'

Hugh shrugged. 'Your captain told me you would both be here. Availability and local knowledge decided the rest, right? He approved the transfer.'

The expression on their mother's face as they entered the house made up for some of the sudden hurt.

Dancer said softly, 'It may be fun, Dick. Your brother has the cut of an experienced officer.'

Bolitho replied grudgingly, 'He has that, damn it!'

Bolitho watched Hugh leading their mother into an adjoining room. When she came out again she was no longer smiling.

'I am so sorry, Dick, and more so for you, Martyn.'

Dancer said firmly, 'You need not be, ma'am. We have both become used to the unexpected.'

'Nevertheless. . . .'

She turned as Hugh entered the room, a glass of brandy in one hand.

'*Nevertheless*, dear family, it is a serious affair. This is just the tip of the berg. God knows what that fool Morgan was about when he was killed, but no revenue man should act alone.' His eyes moved to Bolitho. 'It is far worse than smuggling. At first we believed it was the foul weather. Wrecks are common enough on this coast.'

Bolitho chilled. So that was it. Wreckers. The worst crime of all.

His brother continued in his clipped tones, 'But we have received news of too many rich cargoes lost of late. Silver and gold, spirits and valuable spices. Enough to feed a city, or raise an army.' He shrugged, as if weary of confidences. 'But my duty is to seek out these murderers and hand them to the authorities. The whys and wherefores are not for a King's officer to determine.'

His mother said huskily, 'But wreckers! How could they? Loot and rob helpless seamen. . . .'

Hugh smiled gently. 'They see their betters reaping a rich bounty from ships run ashore on their private land. Reason soon flies out of the window, Mother.'

Dancer protested, 'But an accidental wreck is a far cry from being lured aground, sir!'

Hugh looked away. 'Possibly. But not to the leeches who live off the trade.'

Dancer said, 'Your presence here will be well known by now, sir.'

Hugh nodded. 'I will warm a few palms, make a few promises. Some will give information just to send the *Avenger* somewhere else!'

Bolitho looked at his friend. This was a different kind of Navy. Where a commanding officer could use bribery to gain information, and then act independently without waiting for ponderous authority to give him its blessing.

The door flew open and Nancy rushed across the

room and threw her arms around her brother's neck.

'Hugh! This really is a gathering of the clan!'

He held her away and studied her for several seconds.

'You are a lady now, well *almost*.' He raised his guard again. 'We'll sail on the tide. I suggest you make your way to the harbour and hail a boat.' His tone hardened. 'Don't fret, Mother, I have become very swift in matters of this sort. We shall have Christmas together if I have anything to say on it!'

As Bolitho closed the door to go to his room he heard his mother's voice.

'But *why*, Hugh? You were doing so well aboard your ship! Everyone said your captain was pleased with your behaviour!'

Bolitho hesitated. Unwilling to eavesdrop, but needing to know what was happening.

Hugh replied shortly, 'I left the *Laertes* and was offered this command. *Avenger*'s not much, but she's mine. I can lend weight and authority to the revenue cutters and excisemen, and do much as I please. I have few regrets.'

'But why did you decide so?'

'Very well, Mother. It was a convenience, if you must know. I had a disagreement. . . .'

Bolitho heard his mother sob and wanted to go to her.

He heard Hugh add, 'A matter of honour.'

'Did you kill someone in a duel? Oh, Hugh, what will your father say?'

Hugh gave a short laugh. 'No, I did not kill him. Just cut him a trifle.'

He must have taken her in his arms for the sobs
were quieter and muffled.

'And Father will *not* know. Unless you tell him, eh?'

Dancer waited at the top of the stairs.

'What is it?'

Bolitho sighed. 'My brother has a quick temper. I
think he has been in trouble over an *affair.*'

Dancer smiled. 'In St James's there is always
someone getting nicked or killed in duels. The King
forbids it.' He shrugged. 'But it goes on just the same.'

They helped each other to pack their chests again.
Mrs Tremayne would only burst into tears if they
asked her to do it, even at the promise of a quick
return.

When they went downstairs again Hugh had
disappeared.

Bolitho kissed his mother, and Dancer took her
hand before saying gently, 'If I never returned here,
ma'am, this one visit would have been a great gift to
me.'

Her chin lifted. 'Thank you, Martyn. You are a
good boy. Take care, both of you.'

Two seamen were at the gates, waiting to carry
their chests to the boat.

Bolitho smiled to himself. Hugh had been that
certain. Confident as ever. *In control.*

As they crossed the square by the inn Dancer
exclaimed, 'Look, Dick, the coach!'

They both stopped and stared at it as it rumbled
off the cobbles and the horn gave a lively blare.

Back to Plymouth. It was even the same coachman
and guard.

Bolitho gave a great sigh. 'We had best get aboard the *Avenger*. I am afraid Mrs Tremayne's cooking has blunted my eagerness for duty.'

They turned towards the sea, and heads bowed made their way on to the jetty.

3

Like a Bird

After a lively crossing to the anchored cutter Bolitho found the *Avenger* surprisingly steady for her size. Holding his hat clapped to his head in the icy wind, he paused by the small companionway while he studied the vessel's solitary mast and the broad deck which shone in the grey light like metal. The bulwarks were pierced on either beam to take ten six-pounders, while both forward and right aft by the taffrail he noticed additional mountings for swivel guns. Small she might be, but no slouch in a fight, he decided.

A figure loomed through a busy throng of working seamen and confronted the two midshipmen. He was a giant in height and girth, with a face so weather-beaten he looked more like a Spaniard than any Briton.

He said loudly, ' 'Eard about you.' He thrust out a big, scarred hand. 'Andrew Gloag, actin' master o' this vessel.'

Bolitho introduced Dancer and watched them

together. The slim, fair midshipman, the great, un-shakable figure in the patched blue coat. Gloag may have begun life in Scotland with a name like his, but his dialect was as Devonian as you could imagine.

'Better lay aft, young gennlemen.' Gloag squinted towards the shore. 'We'll be weighin' presently, if the cap'n is anything to judge by.' He grinned, revealing several gaps in his teeth. 'I 'opes you're not too much like '*im*. I can't stand a brace o' you!' He laughed and pushed them towards the companion. 'Get below an' see to yer gear.' He swung away, cupping his hands to bellow, 'Look alive, you idle bugger! Catch a turn with that line or I'll skin you for supper!'

Bolitho and Dancer clambered breathlessly down a short ladder and groped their way to a small stern cabin, banging their heads more than once on the low deckhead beams. The *Avenger* seemed to enfold them with her own sounds and smells. Some familiar and some less so. She felt like a workboat more than a man-of-war. In a class all of her own. Like Andrew Gloag, whose loud voice carried easily through wind and stout timbers alike. A master's mate and acting master. He might never command the quarterdeck of a ship like *Gorgon*, but here he was a king.

It was hard to picture him working with Hugh. He thought suddenly of his brother, wondering, as he often did, why he felt that he never really knew him.

Hugh was changed in some ways. Harder, more confident, if that were possible. More to the point, he was unhappy.

Dancer pushed his chest into a vacant corner and

sat on it, his head almost reaching one of the deck beams.

'What do you make of it all, Dick?'

Bolitho listened to the creak and groan of timbers, the rattle and slap of wet rigging somewhere overhead. It would get more lively once they cleared the Roads.

'Wrecking, smuggling, I believe the two always go hand in hand, Martyn. But the port admiral at Plymouth must have heard more than we, if he's so willing to send the *Avenger*.'

'I heard your brother say that he had lost his senior by putting him in a prize, Dick. I wonder what happened to the cutter's last commander?' He smiled. 'Your brother seems to have a way of getting rid of people.' The smile vanished. 'I am sorry. That was a stupid thing to say!'

Bolitho touched his sleeve. 'No. You're right. He does have that way with him.'

Oars thrashed alongside, accompanied by more curses and threats from Mr Gloag.

'Jolly boat's away again.' Bolitho grimaced. 'Hugh'll be coming aboard now.'

It took Lieutenant Hugh Bolitho longer than expected to return to his command. When he did arrive he was drenched in spray, grim-faced and obviously in ill humour.

In the cabin he threw himself down on a bench and snapped, 'When I come aboard I expect to be met by my officers.' He glared at the midshipmen. 'This is no ship of the line with ten men for each trivial task. This is. . . .' He swung round on the bench as a frightened looking seaman peered in at them. 'Where the *hell* have you been, Warwick?' He did not wait for a reply. 'Bring some brandy and something hot to go with it.' The man fled.

In a calmer tone he continued, 'In a King's ship, no matter how small, you must always keep up an example.'

Bolitho said, 'I'm sorry. I thought as we are only *attached* to your command. . . .'

Hugh smiled. 'Attached, pressed, volunteered, I don't care which. You're both my officers until the word says otherwise. There's work to do.'

He looked up as Gloag came through the door, his great frame doubled over like a weird hunchback.

'Sit you down, Mr Gloag. We'll take a glass before we set sail. All well?'

The master removed his battered hat, and Bolitho saw with surprise he was quite bald, like a brown egg, with the hair at his neck and cheeks as thick as spunyarn as if to compensate for his loss.

Hugh said, 'You will assume duties of second-in-command, Richard. Mr Dancer will assist you. Two halves to make the whole, eh?' He smiled at his joke.

Gloag seemed to sense the atmosphere and rumbled, 'I 'eard that you took command of a brig, the pair of you, when your lieutenants were too sick or injured to be of use?'

Dancer nodded, his eyes shining. 'Aye, sir. The *Sandpiper*. Dick took command like a veteran!'

Hugh said, 'Good, here's the brandy.' Half to himself he added, 'We want no heroes cluttering *these* decks, thank you.'

Bolitho looked at his friend and winked. They had scored a small victory over Hugh's sarcasm.

He asked, 'What about the smugglers, Mr Gloag?'

'Oh, this an' that. Spirits and spices, silks and other such nonsense for them with too much money. Mr Pyke says we'll soon 'ave 'em by the 'eels.'

Dancer looked at him. 'Pyke?'

Hugh Bolitho pushed some goblets across a low table. 'Pyke's my boatswain. Used to be a preventative officer himself before he got more sense and signed to wear the King's coat.' He held up his goblet. 'Welcome, gentlemen.'

The nervous seaman named Warwick, who was also the cabin servant, carried in a lighted lantern and hung it carefully on a beam.

Bolitho had his goblet to his lips when he saw Dancer's eyes flash a quick warning. He looked down and saw a dark stain on Hugh's stocking. He had seen too much of it in the last year not to recognize blood. For an instant longer he imagined Hugh was injured, or had snared his leg climbing aboard. Then he saw his brother meeting his gaze with a mixture of defiance and need.

Feet thudded overhead, and then Hugh placed his goblet very carefully on the table.

'You will work watch-and-watch. Once we have cleared the headland we will run to the south'rd and find some sea-room. I have information, but not enough. Show no lights and pass no unnecessary commands. My people know their work, and most of them are ex-fishermen and the like, as sure-footed as cats. I want to run these smugglers or wreckers to ground without delay, before it becomes catching hereabouts. It has happened in the past. Even in times of war the *trade* has been busy in both directions, they tell me.'

Gloag groped for his hat and went stooping towards the door. 'I'll get things ready, sir.'

Hugh glanced at Dancer. 'Go with him. Learn your way around the deck. She's no *Gorgon*.' As Dancer made his way towards the door, his shadow swaying about with the pitching lantern, he added softly, 'Or *Sandpiper* either, for that matter!'

Alone for the first time the brothers studied each other.

Bolitho thought he could see through Hugh's scornful guard. He was stiff with the authority of his first, if perhaps temporary, command. But at twenty-one, with only himself to answer, that was understandable. But there was anxiety there also, a defensive hardness in his eyes.

He did not have to wait for long.

Hugh said offhandedly, 'You saw this stain? Pity. But can't be helped, I suppose. I can trust you to stay silent?'

Bolitho matched his mood, keeping his face and tone level and impassive.

'Need you ask?'

'No. I'm sorry.' He reached for the brandy and poured another goblet, the movement without conscious thought. 'A matter I had to settle.'

'Here? In Falmouth?' Bolitho almost got to his feet. 'What about Mother?'

Hugh sighed. 'It was partly because of her. It was

some fool who wanted revenge over another affair.'

'The *affair* which had you removed from *Laertes*?'

'Yes.' His eyes were distant. 'He wanted money. So I answered his insults in the only honourable way.'

'You provoked him.' He watched for some hint of guilt. 'Then you killed him.'

Hugh took out his watch and held it to the lantern.

'Well, the second part is correct, damn him!'

Bolitho shook his head. 'One day you'll put a foot wrong.'

Hugh smiled fully for the first time. It was as if he were glad, relieved to have shared his secret.

'Well, until that sad day, young Richard, there is work to be done. So get yourself on deck and rouse the hands. We'll up-anchor before we lose the light. I don't want to end up in splinters across St Anthony Head because of you!'

The weather had worsened considerably, and as Bolitho climbed up through the hatch he felt the punch of the wind like a fist. Figures bustled this way and that, bare feet slapping on the wet planking like so many seals. Despite the wind and soaking spray, the men wore only their checkered shirts and white, flapping trousers, and were apparently unmoved by the bitter weather.

Bolitho ducked aside as the jolly boat was swayed up and over the lee bulwark, showering the men who worked the tackles with more icy water. He saw the boatswain, Pyke, directing the operations until the boat was securely made fast on her tier, and could well imagine him as a revenue man. He had a furtive, even sly, look, and was quite unlike any boatswain he had ever seen.

It would take some getting used to, he thought. Men everywhere, loosening belaying pins and checking the many flaked lines and halliards as if expecting them to be frozen.

It would be dark early, and the nearest land looked indistinct and blurred, the ramparts at Pendennis and St Mawes already without shape or identity.

Gloag was shouting, 'Three men to the tiller! She'll be lively as a parson's daughter when she comes about, lads!'

Bolitho heard someone laugh. That was always a good sign. Gloag might be fearsome, but he was quite obviously respected too.

Dancer said quickly, 'Here comes our captain, Dick.'

Bolitho turned as his brother came on deck. In spite of the weather he was without a cloak or even a tarpaulin coat to protect himself. The lapels of his lieutenant's coat were very white in the dull murk around him, and he wore his cocked hat at a slightly rakish angle, like a figure in an unnamed painting.

Bolitho touched his hat. 'The master informs me we are ready to get under way, sir.' He was surprised the formality came so easily. But it was the Navy speaking. Not one brother to another.

'Very well. Break out the anchor, if you please. Send the hands to their stations. We'll get the main and fore on her as soon as we weigh and see how she takes 'em. Once clear of the headland I'll want jib and tops'l set.'

'Reefed, sir?'

The eyes steadied on him for a moment. 'We shall see.'

Bolitho hurried towards the blunt bows. It seemed incredible that *Avenger* could set so much canvas on one mast and in this sort of wind.

He listened to the metallic clink of pawls as the men at the capstan threw their weight on the bars. He pictured the anchor, it's fluke biting into the sea bed, waiting to break free, free of the land. He often thought of it at times like this.

He jerked out of his thoughts as his brother called sharply, 'Mr Bolitho! More hands to the mains'l! It will be fierce work directly!'

Gloag was banging his big hands together like boards. 'Wind's backed a piece, sir!' He was grinning into the blown spray, his cheeks streaming. 'That'll help!'

Bolitho climbed over unfamiliar gun tackles and thick snakes of cordage. Past unknown seamen and petty officers, until he was right above the stem. He saw the straining cable, jerking inboard through the hawse-hole as more men took the strain, while on either side of the stem the tide surged past as if the *Avenger* herself was already moving ahead.

The boatswain dashed forward to join him. 'A good night for it, sir!' He did not bother to explain but made a circling motion with his fist and yelled, '*Hove short, sir!*'

Then everything seemed to happen as once. As the anchor started to drag free of the ground the hands on deck threw themselves to the big boomed mainsail as if their lives depended on it. Bolitho had to jump clear as the foresail was broken free and started to billow into the wind, only to be knocked aside again as Pyke yelled, '*Anchor's aweigh, sir!*'

The effect was immediate and startling. With her fore and main filling out like mad things, and the deck canting steeply to the thrust of wind and current, the *Avenger* seemed to be sliding beam-on towards sure destruction.

Gloag called hoarsely, 'Sheet 'em 'ome '*ard*, Mr Pyke! Lively now.'

Bolitho felt at a loss and totally in the way as men darted hither and thither, oblivious to the water which surged as high as the lee gunports.

And then, just as suddenly, it was done. Bolitho made his way aft to where three straddle-legged seamen stood by the long tiller-bar, their eyes squinting in concentration as they watched both helm and sails. The *Avenger* was standing as close to the wind as any vessel he had ever seen, with her big mainsail and the fin-shaped foresail sheeted home as Gloag had ordered, until they were almost fore and aft along the cutter's centre line.

Foam boiled under the counter, and Bolitho saw Dancer watching him from the foredeck, grinning like a boy with a new plaything.

Hugh was eyeing him too, his mouth compressed in a tight line.

'Well?' One word. Question and threat together.

Bolitho nodded. 'She's a lady, sir! Like a bird!'

The boatswain stumped to the weather rail and peered at the blurred shoreline.

'Aye, Mr Bolitho, sir. An' I'll wager some devils are watchin' this bird right now!'

The land was edging past, and Bolitho saw the spray whipped off the wave crests like spume as they approached the dangerous turn of the headland.

Pyke cupped his hands. 'Stand by to get aloft, there!' He glanced at his commander's set features as if expecting him to cancel his demands for more canvas. When no word was uttered he added heartily, 'An' mebbe a tot for the first one down afterwards!'

Bolitho made himself take in the darkening deck section by section, until he could match what he already knew with the bustling seamen and the jumble of rigging and blocks which went to make a vessel stay alive.

Hugh and the master seemed satisfied, he thought, watching the men at work, the set of the sails, with an occasional glance at the compass to confirm some point or other.

What a step I have yet to make, Bolitho thought. From midshipman to a place on the quarterdeck. Like his brother, who at twenty-one was already on another plane. In a few years this first, tiny command would probably be forgotten, and Hugh might have his own frigate. But she would have played her vital part for him all the same. Provided, that was, he kept out of trouble and held his sword in its scabbard.

'*Mr Bolitho!*'

Hugh's voice made him start.

'I said earlier, we have no passengers in my command! So stir yourself and put more hands forrard to the jib. We'll set it as soon as the topmen are aloft.'

As dusk yielded to a deeper darkness the *Avenger* threw herself across the stiffer crests of open sea. Lifting and plunging, throwing up great sheets of spray from her bows, she changed tack to point her stem towards the south.

Hour after hour, Hugh Bolitho drove every one until he was ready to drop. Wet, freezing canvas, iron-hard and unyielding to the fingers of salt-blinded men, drowned even the sea's noise with its constant boom and thunder. The screech of blocks as swollen cordage was hauled through, the stamp of feet on deck, an occasional cry from the poop, all joined in one chorus of effort and pain.

Even the cutter's young commander had to admit that too much canvas was too much, and reluctantly he ordered the topsail and jib to be taken in for the remainder of the night.

Eventually the watch below, gasping and bruised, groped their way down for a short respite. Some swore they would never set foot aboard again once they put into port. They always said it. They usually came back.

Others were too tired even to think, but fell on their cramped messdeck to lie amongst the sluicing mixture of sea water and oddments of clothing or loose tackle until the next call from the deck.

'All hands! All hands on deck to shorten sail!' They never had to wait long for that either.

As he lay in a makeshift cot, pitching and swaying with the savage motion, Bolitho found time to wonder what might have happened if he had gone to London as Dancer had suggested.

There was a smile on his lips as he fell into a deep sleep. It would certainly have been totally different from this, he thought.

4

No Choice

Lieutenant Hugh Bolitho sat wedged into a corner of the *Avenger*'s low cabin, one foot against a frame to hold himself steady. The cutter was alive with creaks and rattles as she drifted sluggishly downwind through a curtain of sleet and snow.

The midshipmen, Gloag, the acting-master, and Pyke, the cutter's sly-faced boatswain, completed the gathering, and the confined space was heavy with damp and the richer tang of brandy.

Bolitho felt as if he had never worn a shred of dry clothing in his life. For over two days, while the *Avenger* had tacked or beaten her way down the Cornish coastline, he had barely slept for more than minutes at a time. Hugh never seemed to rest. He was always calling for extra vigilance, although who but a madman would be abroad in this weather was hard to fathom. Now, around the dreaded Lizard and its great sprawl of reefs, they lay to under the lee of the shore. And although it was pitch-dark and no land in view, they sensed it, felt it not as a friend but as a treacherous enemy waiting to rip out their keel if they made just one mistake.

Bolitho was impressed by his brother's outward calm, the way he outlined his ideas without any sign of uncertainty. He could tell that Gloag trusted his judgement, although he was old enough to be his father.

He was saying, 'I had intended to put a party ashore, or go myself to meet this informant. However, the weather has other ideas. Any boat might lose her way, and the advantage of surprise would also be lost.'

Bolitho glanced at Dancer, wondering if he was as mystified as himself. Informants, stealthy rendezvous in the dark, it was a different sort of Navy.

Pyke said abruptly, 'I knows the place well, sir. It would be where Morgan, the revenue man, was done in. A real likely spot for runnin' a cargo ashore.'

Hugh's eyes settled on him curiously. 'D'you think you could meet this fellow? After all, if he says the birds have flown there's no damn point in my hanging about here.'

Pyke spread his hands. 'I can try, sir.'

'*Try*, dammit, that's not good enough!'

Bolitho watched. Again, Hugh's latent temper was getting the better of him. He saw the almost physical effort as reason took over.

The lieutenant added, 'You do see what I mean?'

'Aye, sir. If we gets ashore without stovin' the boat's bottom in, we could reach 'is cottage as you wanted in the first place.'

Hugh nodded briskly. 'Very well. I want you to

land the party as soon as you can. Find out what the man knows, but pay him nothing. We've got to be sure.' He looked at his brother. 'You, Richard, will go with Mr Pyke. The presence of my, er, second-in-command will add something, eh?'

Gloag rubbed his bald pate. 'I'll go an' check the set o' the tide, sir. We don't want to lose your brother on 'is first affray, does we?' He went out chuckling to himself.

His chuckling stopped as a voice called, 'Breakers on the lee bow, sir!' That was Truscott, the gunner, standing a watch alone while his betters pondered on matters of strategy.

Hugh Bolitho said, 'Too many reefs about here. Take yourself on deck, Mr Dancer. Have the jolly boat swayed out and muster the landing party. See that they are armed, but ensure that nobody steps into the boat with a loaded piece. I want no eager hands loosing off a pistol by mistake.' His eyes flashed. 'You'll be answerable to me.'

He relaxed slightly. 'It is all we can do. They say that a cargo of smuggled goods has been dropped in the next cove to the nor'-west of where I am putting you ashore. They say it will stay there until everyone believes the *Avenger* elsewhere.' He banged the table. 'They *say* a lot of things, but tell me nothing of value!'

Pyke grinned. 'It sounds right, sir. I'll take the centipedes, just in case.'

Another voice called, 'Boat ready, zur! Mr Gloag's respects, an' could the young gentleman make haste?'

Hugh nodded. 'Immediately.' He led the way on deck.

Bolitho felt the damp biting into his bones. Easy living for a few days at home had had its effects, he thought ruefully. Now, tired and weary from the sea and wind, he was feeling very low indeed.

He peered at the tossing boat alongside. It was so dark he could barely make out its outline, just a pitching shape in a welter of white spray.

Dancer hurried to his side. 'I wish I was going with you.'

Bolitho gripped his arm. 'Me too. I feel a complete novice amongst these people.'

His brother lurched across the slippery planking. 'Be off with you. Carry on, Bosun.' He waited for Pyke to vanish over the side and added quietly, 'Keep your eyes wide open. I will lie to when I can, but in any case will be nearby at first light. If there is any truth in my information we may stand a chance.'

Bolitho threw his leg over the bulwark and waited for his eyes to adjust to the darkness. One false step and he would be swept away like a wood chip on a mill-race.

The boat cast off and veered away from the *Avenger* almost before he had regained his breath, while Pyke swung the tiller-bar and peered above the oarsmen's heads as if to seek a way through the nearest line of leaping breakers.

To calm his nerves Bolitho asked, 'What are the centipedes, Mr Pyke?'

The stroke oarsman grinned, his teeth very white in the darkness. ' 'Ere, sir!' He kicked out with his foot as he leaned aft for another pull at his oar.

Bolitho reached down and felt two enormous grapnels. They were unlike any he had seen, with several sets of flukes like legs.

Pyke did not take his eyes from the shore as he said, 'The smugglers usually sink their booty to wait until the coast is clear. Then they lifts it when they'm good and ready. My little centipedes can drag the stuff off the bottom.' He laughed quietly, a humourless sound. 'I've done a few in me time.'

The bowman called, 'Land ahead, sir!'

The boat was planing forward, the spray hissing between the oar blades to beat across the already dripping inmates.

'Easy, all!'

A tall, slab-sided rock rushed down the starboard side, muffling the sound of breakers like a huge door.

With a lurch and a violent shudder the boat grounded on hard sand, and as men fell cursing in the water and tried to steady the impact, others leapt on to the beach to guide the bows clear of fallen rocks.

Bolitho tried to stop his teeth chattering. He had to assume Gloag and Pyke knew what they were doing, that his brother's plan made sense. This was the cove, but to Bolitho it could have been anywhere.

Pyke regarded him through the gloom. 'Well, sir?'

'You know this business better than me.'

Bolitho knew some of the men were listening, but this was no time to stand on dignity at the expense of safety. He was *Avenger*'s second-in-command. But he was a lowly midshipman for all that.

Pyke grunted, satisfied or contemptuous it was impossible to say.

He said, 'Two men stand by the boat. Load your weapons now.' He gestured upwards into the darkness. 'Ashmore, you stand guard. Watch out for any nosey bugger hanging around.'

The invisible Ashmore asked, 'An' if I does, sir?'

'Crack 'is 'ead, for Gawd's sake!'

Pyke adjusted his belt. 'The rest of you, come with us.' To Bolitho he added, 'Night like this, should be all right.'

The snow swirled around them as they fumbled their way up a winding, treacherous pathway. Once, Bolitho paused to give a seaman his hand on a slippery piece of the track and saw the sea reaching out far below him. Impenetrable black lined with broken crests of incoming rollers.

He thought of his mother. It was unreal to know that she was only twelve miles or so away from where he was standing. But there was a world of difference between a straight bird's flight and the *Avenger*'s meandering track to this particular point.

Pyke was tireless, and his long, thin legs were taking him up the path as if they did it every single day.

Bolitho tried to ignore the cold and the blinding sleet. It was like walking into oblivion.

He collided with Pyke's back as the boatswain hissed, '*Still!* Th' cottage is up 'ere, somewhere.'

Bolitho fingered his sheathed hanger and strained his ears, expecting to hear something.

Pyke nodded. 'This way.' He hurried on again, the track levelling off as the little group of men left the sea behind them.

The cottage loomed out of the sleet like a pale rock. It was little more than the size of a large room, Bolitho thought, with very low walls, some kind of thatched roof and small, sightless windows.

Who would want to live here? he wondered. It must be quite a walk to the nearest hamlet or village.

Pyke was peering at the little cottage with professional interest. To Bolitho he said, 'Man's name is Portlock. Bit of everything 'e is. Poacher, crimp for the press gangs, 'e can turn 'is 'and to most trades.' He laughed shortly. ' 'Ow 'e's escaped the noose all these years I'll not know.' He sighed. 'Robins, go 'alf a cable along the track and watch out. Coote, round the back. There's no door, but you never knows.' He looked at Bolitho. 'Better if you knocks the door.'

'But I thought we were supposed to be quiet about it?'

'Up to a point. We've come this far safe an' sound.' He approached the cottage calmly. 'But if we are bein' watched, Mr Bolitho, we got to make it look good, or Mister bloody Portlock will soon be gutted like a fish!'

Bolitho nodded. He was learning.

Then he drew his curved hanger and after a further hesitation he banged it sharply on the door.

For a moment longer nothing happened. Just the patter of sleet across the thatch and their wet clothing, the irregular breathing of the seamen.

Then a voice called, 'W-who be it at this hour?'

Bolitho swallowed hard. He had been expecting a gruff voice to match Pyke's description. But it was a female. Young by the sound of her, and frightened too.

He heard the rustle of expectancy from the sailors and said firmly, 'Open the door, ma'am. In the King's name!'

Slowly and reluctantly the door was pulled back, a shuttered lantern barely making more than a soft orange glow across their feet.

Pyke pushed past impatiently and said, 'One of you stay outside.' He snatched the lantern and fiddled with it, adding, 'Like a bloody tomb!'

Bolitho held his breath as the light spread out from the lantern and laid the cottage bare.

Even in the poor light he could see it was filthy. Old casks and boxes littered the floor, while pieces of flotsam and driftwood were piled against the walls and around the dying fire like a barricade.

Bolitho looked at the girl who had opened the door. She was dressed in little more than rags, and her feet, despite the cold earth floor, were bare. He felt sick. She was about Nancy's age, he thought.

The man, whom he guessed was Portlock, was standing near the rear wall. He was exactly as Bolitho had imagined. Brutal, coarse-featured, a man who would do anything for money.

He exclaimed thickly, 'Oi done nothin'! What right be yours to come a-burstin' in 'ere?'

When nobody answered he became braver and seemingly larger.

He shouted, 'An' what sort o' officer are *you*?'

He glared at Bolitho, his eyes filled with such hatred and evil that he could almost feel the man's strength.

'Oi'll not take such from no *boy*!'

Pyke crossed the room like a shadow. The first blow brought Portlock gasping to his knees, the second knocked him on to his side, a thread of scarlet running from his chin.

Pyke was not even out of breath. 'There now. We understand each other, eh?' He stood back, balanced on his toes, as Portlock rose groaning from the floor. 'In future you will treat a King's officer with respect, no matter what age 'e's at, see?'

Bolitho felt that things were getting beyond him. 'You know why we are here.' He saw the eyes watching him, changing from fury to servility in seconds.

'Oi 'ad to be *certain*, young sir.'

Bolitho turned away, angry and sickened. 'Oh, ask him, for God's sake.'

He looked down as a hand touched his arm. It was the girl, feeling his sodden coat, crooning to herself like a mother to a child.

A seaman said harshly, 'Stand away, girl!' To Bolitho he added vehemently, 'I seen that look afore, sir. When they strips the clothes off the poor devils on the gibbet!'

Pyke said smoothly, 'Or off those unlucky enough to be shipwrecked, eh?'

Portlock said, 'Oi don't know nothin' about that, sir!'

'We shall see.' Pyke regarded the man coldly. 'Tell me, is the cargo still there?'

Portlock nodded, his gaze on the boatswain like a stricken rabbit. 'Aye.'

'Good. And when will they come for it?' His tone sharpened. 'No lies now.'

'Tomorrow mornin'. On th' ebb.'

Pyke looked at Bolitho. 'I believe him. At low tide it's easier to get the cargo 'ooked.' He grimaced. 'Also, it keeps the revenue boats in deeper water.'

Bolitho said, 'We had better get the men together.'

But Pyke was still watching the other man. Eventually he said, 'You will stay 'ere.'

Portlock protested, 'But me money! I was promised. . . .'

'Damn your money!' Bolitho could not stop himself even though he knew Pyke was looking at him with something like amusement. 'If you betray us your fate will be as certain as that meted out by those you are betraying now!'

He looked at the girl, seeing the bruise on her cheek, the cold sores on her mouth. But when he reached out to comfort her she recoiled, and would have spat at him but for a burly seaman's intervention.

Pyke walked out of the cottage and mopped his face. 'Save yer sympathy, Mr Bolitho. Scum breeds on scum.'

Bolitho fell in step beside him. Broadsides and towering pyramids of canvas in a ship of the line seemed even further away now. This was squalor at its lowest, where even the smallest decency was regarded as weakness.

He heard himself say, 'Let us be about it then. I want no more of this place.'

The sleety snow swirled down to greet them, and

when he glanced back Bolitho saw that the cottage had disappeared.

'This be as good a place to wait as any.' Pyke rubbed his hands together and then blew on them. It was the first time he had shown any discomfort.

Bolitho felt his shoes sinking into slush and half-frozen grass, and tried not to think of Mrs Tremayne's hot soup or one of her bedtime possets. Only this was real now. For over two hours they had wended their way along the cliffs, conscious of the wind as it tried to push them into some unknown darkness, of the wretched cold, of their complete dependence on Pyke.

Pyke said, 'The cove is yonder. Not much to look at, but 'tis well sheltered, an' some big rocks 'ide the entrance from all but the nosiest. At low water it'll be firm an' shelvin'.' He nodded, his mind made up. 'That's when it will be. Or another day.'

One of the seamen groaned, and the boatswain snarled, 'What d'you expect? A warm 'ammock and a gallon o' beer?'

Bolitho steeled himself and sat down on a hummock of earth. On either side his small party of seamen, seven in all, arranged themselves as best they could. Three more with the jolly boat somewhere behind them. It was not much of a force if things went wrong. On the other hand, these were all professional seamen. Hard, disciplined, ready for a fight.

Pyke took out a bottle from his coat and passed it to Bolitho. 'Brandy.' He shook with a silent laugh.

'Yer brother took it off a smuggler a while back.'

Bolitho swallowed and held his breath. It was like fire, but found just the right place.

Pyke offered, 'You can pass it along. We've quite a wait yet.'

Bolitho heard the bottle going from hand to hand, the grunts of approval with each swallow.

He forgot the discomfort instantly as he exclaimed, 'I heard a shot!'

Pyke snatched the bottle and thrusting it into his coat said uneasily, 'Aye. A small piece.' He blinked into the darkness. 'A vessel. Out there somewheres. Must be in distress.'

Bolitho chilled even more. Wrecks dotted this shoreline in plenty. Ships from the Caribbean, from the Mediterranean, everywhere. All those leagues of ocean, and then on the last part of the voyage home, Cornwall.

Rocks to rip out a keel, angry cliffs to deny safety to even the strongest swimmer.

And now, after what he had heard, the additional horror of wreckers.

Perhaps he had been mistaken, but even as he tried to draw comfort from the thought another bang echoed against the cliffs and around the hidden cove.

A seaman whispered fiercely, 'Lost 'er way most like. Mistook the Lizard for Land's End. It's 'appened afore, sir.'

Pyke grunted, 'Poor devils.'

'What will we do?' Bolitho tried to see his face. 'We can't just leave them to die.'

'We don't *know* she'll come aground. An' if she

does, we can't be sure she'll sink. She might beach 'erself up at Porthleven, or drift free of danger.'

Bolitho turned away. God, Pyke does not care. All he is interested in is this job. A quick capture with the booty.

He pictured the unknown vessel. Probably carrying passengers. He might even know some of them.

He stood up. 'We will go round the cove, Mr Pyke. We can stand by on the other headland. She'll most likely be in sight very soon.'

Pyke jumped to his feet. 'It's no use, I tell you!' He was almost beside himself with anger. 'What's done is done. The cap'n gave us orders. We must obey 'em.'

Bolitho swallowed hard, feeling them all looking at him.

'Robins, go and tell the men at the boat what we are doing. Can you find the way?'

It only needed Robins to say no, to proclaim ignorance, and it was over before it had started. He could barely recall the other men's names.

But Robins said brightly, 'Aye, sir. I knows it.' He hesitated. 'What then, sir?'

Bolitho said, 'Remain with them. If you sight *Avenger* at daybreak you must make some effort to tell my, er, the captain what we are about.'

It was done. He had disobeyed Hugh's orders, overruled Pyke and taken it on himself to look for the drifting vessel. They had nothing but their weapons, not even one of Pyke's centipedes to grapple the vessel into safer waters.

Pyke said scornfully, 'Follow me then. But I want it understood. I'm dead against it.'

They started to scramble along another narrow path, each wrapped in his own thoughts.

Bolitho thought of the brig *Sandpiper* where he and Dancer had faced a pirate ship twice her size. This was entirely different, and he wished yet again his friend was with him.

As they rounded a great pile of broken rocks a seaman said hoarsely, 'There, sir! Lights!'

Bolitho looked, stunned even though he had been expecting it. Two lanterns, far apart and lower down the sloping side of the headland. They were moving, but only slowly, one hardly at all.

Pyke said, 'Got 'em tied to ponies, I expect. That ship's master out there will think they're ridin' lights.' He spat out the words. 'A safe anchorage.'

Bolitho could see it. As if it had happened. As if he were there. The ship, which seconds before had been beset with doubts and near panic. Then the sight of the two riding lights. Other vessels safely at anchor.

When in fact there was nothing but rocks, and the only hands waiting on the shore would be gripping knives and clubs.

He said, 'We must get to those lights. There may still be time.'

Pyke retorted, 'You must be mad! There's no doubt a bloody army o' the devils down there! What chance do we 'ave?'

Bolitho faced him, surprised at his own voice. Calm, while his whole body was shaking. 'Probably none, Mr Pyke. But we have no choice either.'

As they started to descend towards the cove even

the night seemed to become quieter. Holding its breath for all of them.

'How long before dawn?'

Pyke glanced at him briefly. 'Too far off to 'elp us.'

Bolitho felt for his pistol and wondered if it would fire. Pyke had read his thoughts. Hoping against hope that with daylight they might see the cutter standing inshore to help them.

He thought of Hugh. What he would have done. He would certainly have had a plan.

He said quietly, 'I'll need two men. We'll go for the lights, while you, Mr Pyke, can take the remaining hands to the hill and cause a diversion.'

Just like that.

Pyke stared at him. 'You don't even know this beach! There's not an inch o' cover. They'll cut you down afore you've gone a pace or two!'

Bolitho waited, feeling his skin sticking to his wet shirt. He would be still colder very shortly. And quite dead.

Pyke had sensed his despair, his determination to do the impossible.

He said abruptly, 'Babbage an' Trillo will be best. They knows these parts. They got no cause to die though.'

The one called Babbage drew his heavy cutlass and ran his thumb along the edge. The second seaman, Trillo, was small and wiry, and favoured a wicked-looking boarding axe.

They both moved away from their companions and stood beside the midshipman. They were used to obeying orders. It was senseless to protest.

Bolitho looked at Pyke and said simply, 'Thank you.'

'Huh!' Pyke beckoned to the others. 'Follow me, men.' To Bolitho he added, 'I'll do what I can.'

Bolitho set his hat firmly on his head, and with his hanger in one hand and the heavy pistol in the other he walked clear of the fallen rocks and on to the wet, firm sand.

He could hear the two seamen squelching along at his heels, but the sounds were almost drowned by his own heartbeats against his ribs.

Then he saw the nearest light, the shadowy outline of a tethered horse, and further along the beach another animal with a lantern tied across its back on a long spar.

It seemed impossible that such a crude ruse would deceive anybody, but from experience Bolitho knew a ship's lookouts often only saw what they wanted to see.

He could see several moving figures, briefly silhouetted against the hissing spray around the nearest rocks. His heart sank, there must be twenty or thirty of them.

The puny crackle of pistol shots echoed down into the cove, and Bolitho guessed that Pyke and his men were doing their part. He heard startled cries from the beach, the clatter of steel as someone dropped a weapon amidst the rocks.

Bolitho said, 'Now, fast as we can!'

He dashed towards the horse, hacking the lantern from its spar so that it fell burning on the wet sand. The horse reared away, kicking with terror, as more shots whined overhead.

Bolitho heard his companions yelling like madmen, saw the seaman, Babbage, hack down a charging figure with his cutlass before running on to cut away the next lantern.

A voice yelled, 'Shoot those buggers down!' Someone else screamed in pain as a stray ball found a mark.

Figures fanned out on every side, advancing slowly, hampered and probably confused by Pyke's pistol fire from the hillside.

One dashed forward, and Bolitho fired, seeing the man's contorted face as the ball flung him backwards on to the beach.

Others pressed in, more daring now that they realized there were only three facing them.

Bolitho locked blades with one, while Babbage, slashing and hacking with his heavy cutlass, fought two men single-handed.

Bolitho could feel his adversary's fury, but found time to hear Trillo give just one frantic cry as he was struck down by a whole group of slashing weapons.

'Damn your eyes!' The man was gasping between his teeth. 'Now you die, you bloody rummager!'

Dazed, his mind and body cringing to the inevitability of death, Bolitho was shocked at his own anger. To die was one thing, but to be mistaken for a revenue man was like the final insult.

He remembered with stark clarity how his father had taught him to defend himself. Twisting his wrist with all his strength he plucked the other man's sword from his hand. As he blundered past him he pointed his hanger and then laid it across his neck and shoulder.

Then something struck the side of his head and he was on his knees, dimly aware that Babbage was trying to stand guard above him, his cutlass hissing through the air like an arrow.

But darkness was closing across his mind, and he felt his cheek grind into the wet sand as he pitched headlong, his body exposed to the nearest thrusting blades.

Soon now. He could hear horses and more shouts through the painful blur in his brain.

His last conscious thought was that he hoped his mother would not see him like this.

5

Bait

Bolitho opened his eyes very slowly. As he did so he groaned, the sound thrusting straight through his aching body, as if from the soles of his feet.

He struggled to remember what had happened, and as realization, like the returning pain in his skull, came flooding back, he stared round with dazed bewilderment.

He was lying on a thick fur rug in front of a roaring log fire, still wearing his soiled uniform, which in the great heat was steaming as if about to burst into flames.

Someone was kneeling behind him, and he saw a girl's scrubbed hands reaching round to support his head, which he knew was bandaged.

She murmured, 'Rest easy, zur.' Over her shoulder she called, 'He's awake!'

Bolitho heard a familiar, booming voice, and saw Sir Henry Vyvyan standing above him, his one eye peering down as he said, '*Awake*, girl, he damn near died on us!'

He bellowed at some invisible servants and then added more calmly, 'God swamp me, boy, that was a damn fool thing to do. Another second and those ruffians would have had your liver on the sand!' He handed a goblet to the girl. 'Give him some of this.' He shook his head as Bolitho tried to swallow the hot drink. 'What *would* I have told yer mother, eh?'

'The others, sir?' Bolitho tried to think clearly, remembering Trillo's cry, his last sound on earth.

Vyvyan shrugged. 'One dead. A damned miracle.' He sounded as if he could still not believe it. 'A handful of men against those devils!'

'I thank you, sir. For saving our lives.'

'Nothin' to it, m'boy.' Vyvyan smiled crookedly, the scar across his face looking even more savage in the shadows. 'I came with my men because I heard the gun. I was out with 'em anyway. The Navy isn't the only intelligence round here, y'know!'

Bolitho lay still and looked straight up at the high ceiling. He could see the girl watching him, her eyes very blue, frowning with concern.

So Vyvyan had known all about it. Hugh should have guessed. But for him they would all be dead.

He asked, 'And the ship, sir?'

'Aground. But safe enough 'til mornin'. I sent your boatswain to take charge.' He tapped his big nose. 'Nice bit of salvage there, I shouldn't wonder, eh?'

A door opened somewhere and a voice said harshly, 'Most of 'em got away, sir. We cut down two, but the rest scattered amongst the rocks an' caves. They'll be miles away by dawn.' He chuckled. 'Caught one of 'em though.'

Vyvyan sounded thoughtful. 'But for the ship, and the need to help these sailors, we might have caught the lot.' He rubbed his chin. 'But still, we'll have a hangin' all the same. Show these scum the old fox is not asleep, eh?'

The door closed just as silently.

'I am sorry, sir. I feel it is all my fault.'

'Nonsense! Did yer duty. Quite right too. Only way.' He added grimly, 'But I'll be havin' a sharp word with yer brother, make no mistake on it!'

The heat of the fire, his exhaustion and the effect of something in the drink made Bolitho fall into a deep sleep. When he awoke again it was morning, the hard wintry light streaming in through the windows of Vyvyan Manor.

Freeing himself from two thick blankets he got gingerly to his feet and stared at himself in a wall mirror. He looked more like a survivor than a victor.

He saw Vyvyan watching him from one of the doorways.

Vyvyan asked, 'Ready, boy? My steward tells me that your vessel is anchored off the cove. I've been up most of the night m'self, so I know how you're feelin'.' He grinned. 'But still, nothin' broken. Just a headache for a few days, eh?'

Bolitho put on his coat and hat. He noticed that both had been cleaned, and someone had mended a rent in one of the sleeves where a blade had missed his arm by less than an inch.

It was a cold, bright morning, with the snow changed to slush and the sky without a trace of cloud. Had the night been like this the ship would have

seen the danger and the smugglers would have
picked up their cargo from the cove.

If . . . if . . . if . . . It was too late now.

Vyvyan's coach dropped him on the narrow coast
road above the headland, and to his astonishment he
saw Dancer and some seamen waiting for him, and
far below, a boat drawn up on the beach.

How different it looked in daylight. He almost
expected to see some corpses, but the beach was
silky smooth, and beyond the cove the anchored
Avenger tugged at her cable with barely a roll.

'Dick! Thank God you're safe!' Dancer ran to meet
him and gripped his arm. 'You look terrible!'

Bolitho gave a painful smile. 'Thanks.'

Together they walked down that same steep path,
and Bolitho saw several burly looking men examining the two lanterns and some discarded weapons.
Excisemen, or merely Vyvyan's retainers it was hard
to say.

Dancer said, 'The captain sent us to get you,
Dick.'

'How is his temper?'

'Surprisingly good. I think the vessel you warned
away from the rocks had a lot to do with it. She's
beached a mile or so from here. Your brother, er,
induced her people to come off, then he put a prize
crew aboard. I think her master was so glad to save
his skin he forgot the matter of prize money!'

By the boat Bolitho saw some seamen replacing
Pyke's centipedes in the sternsheets.

Dancer explained, 'We made a drag along the sea-
bed but found nothing. They must have come in the

night after Vyvyan's men had driven away the wreckers.'

Avenger's other boat was already alongside when Bolitho returned on board. The man he had chosen to warn the jolly boat had done well, he thought. Poor Trillo had been their one loss.

Hugh was watching him as he climbed up over the side, hands on hips, hat at the same rakish angle.

'Quite the little fire-brand, aren't you?' He strode across the broad deck and gripped his hand. 'Young idiot. But I guessed you'd disobey my orders as soon as I heard that distress cannon. I had a prize crew aboard before they could say knife.' He smiled. 'Nice little Dutch brig bound for Cork. Spirits and tobacco. Fetch a good price.'

'Sir Henry said the wreckers got away. All but one.'

'Wreckers, smugglers, I believe they're one and the same. Pyke thinks he may have wounded a few with his pistol shots, so they may turn up somewhere. No Cornish jury will ever convict a smuggler, but a wrecker is something else.'

Bolitho faced his brother. 'The loss of the smugglers' cargo was my fault. But I couldn't help myself. A few kegs of brandy against the value of a vessel and her people made me act as I did.'

Hugh nodded gravely. 'As I knew it would. But brandy? I think not. My men found some oiled wrapping hidden away in one of the caves while they were looking for clues. That drop was not for drinking, my brother. It was made up of good French muskets, if I'm any judge.'

Bolitho stared at him. 'Muskets?'

'Aye. For rebellion somewhere, who can say. Ireland, America, there's money a-plenty for anyone who can supply weapons in these troubled times.'

Bolitho shook his head and immediately regretted it. 'It is beyond me.'

His brother rubbed his hands. 'Mr Dancer! My compliments to the master, and tell him to get the vessel under way. If weapons are the bait we need, then weapons we will have.'

Dancer watched him warily. 'And where are we bound, sir?'

'*Bound?* Falmouth of course. I'll not run back to the admiral now. This is getting interesting.' He paused beside the companionway. 'Now get yourself washed and properly turned out, *Mr* Bolitho. I daresay you had a quieter night than some.'

Avenger returned to Falmouth without anything further unusual happening. Once at anchor, Hugh Bolitho went ashore, while Gloag and the midshipmen prepared to take on stores and ward off the curious and others who had obviously been sent out to discover as much information as they could.

Bolitho began to imagine a smuggler at each corner and behind every cask. The news of a shipwreck, and Vyvyan's chase of the would-be wreckers had preceded *Avenger*'s arrival, and there would be plenty of speculation as to what would happen next.

When the cutter's young commander returned he was in unusual good humour.

In the cabin he said, 'All done. I have had words with certain people in town. The story will be that

Avenger is out searching for another arms runner in the channel. By this ruse, the smugglers on this side will know we have discovered about the muskets, even though we did not find any ourselves.' He looked cheerfully from Gloag to his brother and then to Dancer. 'Well? Don't you see? It's almost perfect.'

Gloag rubbed his bald head as he always did when he was considering something doubtful, and answered, 'I can well see that nobody'll know for certain about another cargo, sir. The Frenchies will keep sendin' 'em once they've a buyer. But where will *we* get such a haul?'

'We won't.' His smile grew broader. 'We'll sail into Penzance and land a cargo of our own. Load it into waggons and send it overland to Truro to the garrison there. The governor of Pendennis has agreed to lend us a tempting cargo of muskets, powder and shot. Along the way to Truro someone will attempt to seize the lot of it. With the roads as they are, how could they resist the temptation?'

Bolitho asked quietly, 'Wouldn't it be wiser to tell the port admiral at Plymouth what you are about first?'

Hugh glared at him. 'From you that is priceless! You know what would happen. He'd either say no, or take so long the whole country would know what we were doing. No, we'll do this quickly and do it well.' He smiled briefly. 'This time.'

Bolitho looked at the deck. An ambush, the anticipation of quick spoils giving way to panic as the attackers realized they were the ones in the trap. And no escape into little caves this time.

Hugh said, 'I have sent word to Truro. The dragoons will be back by now. The colonel is a friend of father's. He'll enjoy this sort of thing. Like pig-sticking!'

There was a sudden silence, and Bolitho found himself thinking of the dead Trillo. They were all here safe and busy. He was already buried and forgotten.

Dancer said, 'I think it would work, sir. It would depend a lot on the people who were watching for an attack.'

'Quite. On a lot of luck too. But we'll have lost nothing by trying. If all else fails, we'll stir up such a hornets' nest that we may push somebody into laying information just to get rid of us!'

A boat grated alongside, and minutes later Pyke entered the cabin.

He took a goblet of brandy with an appreciative nod and said, 'The prize is in the 'ands of the Chief Revenue Officer, sir. All taken care of.' He glanced at Bolitho and added, 'That informer, Portlock. 'E's dead, by the way, sir. Somebody talked too loud.'

Hugh Bolitho asked, 'Another glass of brandy, anybody?'

Bolitho looked at him grimly. Hugh knew already. Must have known all along that the man would be killed.

He asked, 'What of the girl?'

Pyke was still studying him. 'Gawn. Good riddance too. Like I said. Scum breeds on scum.'

Hornets' nest, his brother had predicted. It was stirring already by the sound of it.

The bell chimed overhead and Hugh Bolitho said, 'I'm for the shore. I'll be dining at the house, Richard.'

He glanced at Dancer. 'Care to join me? I think my brother had best remain aboard until he's free of that bandage. Mother will have vapours if she sees our hero like that!'

Dancer looked at Bolitho. 'No, sir. I'll remain here.'

'Good. Stand a good watch at all times. There'll be quite a few tongues wagging in the Falmouth ale houses tonight, I shouldn't wonder.'

As he climbed up from the cabin and left the two midshipmen alone, Bolitho said, 'You should have gone, Martyn. Nancy would have liked it.'

Dancer smiled ruefully. 'We came together. We'll stay that way. After last night, I think you need a bodyguard, Dick!'

Gloag came back from seeing his captain over the side and picked up his goblet. In his fist it looked like a thimble.

'What I want to know is,' he eyed them fiercely, 'what 'appens if they knows what we're up to? If they've got ears and eyes amongst us already?'

Bolitho stared at him, but Dancer answered first.

'Then, Mr Gloag, sir, I fear the loss of government arms and powder will take more explaining than we are capable of.'

Gloag nodded heavily. 'My thought too.' He took another swallow and smacked his lips. 'Very nasty it could be.'

Bolitho thought of what the admiral at Plymouth and his own captain in the *Gorgon* would have to say about it.

The careers of James Bolitho's two sons might come to a speedy end.

6

A Plain Duty

Bolitho wandered up and down the high stone jetty
and watched the activity of Penzance harbour. But
for the bitter cold it could almost have been spring, he
thought. The colours of the moored fishing boats and
grubby coasting vessels, the rooftops and church spires
of the town beyond the anchorage seemed brighter
and more cheerful than they should have been.

He looked down at the *Avenger* tied to the jetty.
She seemed even less a King's ship from this angle.
Her broad deck was strewn with ropes and alive with
bustling seamen. But here and there he saw the
occasional motionless figure. Watchful, despite the
casual atmosphere, ready to seek out any suspicious
loiterer nearby.

Even their departure had been well planned and
executed with stealth. The cargo of borrowed arms
and powder had been swayed aboard in total darkness, while Pyke and over twenty hands had pat-
rolled the nearest jetty and street, just to be sure that
nobody had seen what they were about.

Then, taking good care to avoid local shipping, *Avenger* had stood away from the land before heading down channel again, towards Penzance.

Hugh was ashore now, as usual leaving neither explanation nor destination.

Bolitho studied the passing men and women, seamen and fisherfolk, traders and idlers. Had the rumour gone out yet? Was someone already plotting a way of ambushing Hugh's fictitious capture?

Dancer clambered up from the cutter and stood beside him, rubbing his hands to ward off the cold.

Bolitho said, 'It *seems* very peaceful, Martyn.'

His friend nodded cheerfully. 'Your brother has thought of everything. The chief revenue officer has been here, and I'm told that waggons are being sent to collect our precious hoard!' His mouth widened to a grin. 'I didn't know the Navy ever got mixed up in this kind of game.'

A seaman called, 'Cap'n's a'comin', sir!'

Bolitho waved to the man. He had grown to like the friendly way that forecastle and afterguard shared their confidences when one might expect such an overcrowded hull to drive them further apart.

Hugh Bolitho, wearing his sword and looking very sure of himself, climbed swiftly down to the deck, the midshipmen following at a respectful distance.

Hugh touched his hat to the poop and briskly flapping ensign and said, 'Waggons will be here presently. They've done well. The whole town's agog with news of our little enterprise. Good muskets and powder, seized from a potential enemy.'

He ran his glance swiftly over the large bundles of

muskets which were already being swayed up from the hold under the gunner's watchful eye.

He sniffed the air. 'Good day to begin too. No hanging about. It's what they will be watching. Probably right now. To see if we're really intent on getting the cargo ashore and into safe hands, or are trailing our coats as a ruse.'

Gloag, who had been listening, said admiringly, 'You've a clever mind an' no mistake, sir. I can see you in your own flagship afore too long!'

'Maybe.' Hugh walked to the companionway. 'The waggons will be loaded and under guard from the moment they arrive. There'll be a party of revenue men as additional escort.' His eyes fixed on Dancer. 'You will be in charge. The senior revenue man will know what to do, but I want a King's officer *in charge*.'

Bolitho said quickly, 'I'll go, sir. It doesn't seem right to send him. It was because of me he is here at all.'

'The matter is closed.' Hugh smiled. 'Besides, it will all be over before you know it. A few bloody heads and the sight of the dragoons will be sufficient. Sir Henry Vyvyan can have all the hangings he wants after that!'

As he vanished below Dancer said, 'It's no matter, Dick. We've done far worse in the old *Gorgon*. And this may stand us in good stead when our examinations come due, whenever that wretched day will be!'

By noon the waggons had arrived and were loaded without delay. Again, Hugh Bolitho had planned it well. Not enough fuss to make the preparations appear false, but enough to suggest the genuine pride of a young commander's capture.

If it went well, Gloag's remark would make good sense. The prize money from the stranded Dutch vessel and the destruction of a gang of smugglers or wreckers would do much to push Hugh's other problems to one side.

'You there! Give me a hand down with my bag!'

Bolitho turned to see a seaman helping a tall, loose-limbed man in a plain blue coat and hat down on to the cutter's bulwark.

The seaman seemed to know him well and grinned. 'Welcome back, Mr Whiffin, sir!'

Bolitho hurried aft, raking through his mind to place where he had heard the name. He had now been aboard the cutter for ten days and had learned the names and duties of most of the men, but Whiffin's role eluded him.

The tall man regarded him calmly. A mournful, expressionless face.

He said, 'Whiffin. Clerk-in-charge.'

Bolitho touched his hat. Of course, that was it. These cutters carried a senior clerk to do several jobs in one. To act as purser, captain's clerk, in some cases even to try their hand at surgery, and Whiffin looked as if he could do all of them. Bolitho remembered hearing his brother mention vaguely he had put Whiffin ashore for some reason or other. Anyway, now he was back.

'Captain aboard?' He was studying Bolitho curiously. 'You'll be the brother then.'

Wherever he had been, Whiffin was remarkably well informed.

'Aft.'

'Very well. I'd better see him.'

Shooting another glance at Dancer he went below, twisting himself around and down the companion like a weasel.

'Well now.' Dancer pursed his lips in a whistle. 'He's a strange one.'

The boatswain's mate of the watch called, 'Cap'n wants you below, sir!'

Bolitho hurried to the ladder, wondering if Whiffin's return had changed something. Perhaps he and not Dancer was going with the waggons after all.

His brother looked up sharply as he entered the cabin. Whiffin was sitting near him, filling the air with smoke from a long clay pipe.

'Sir?'

'Slight alteration, Richard.' He gave a small smile. 'I want you to get ashore and find the chief revenue officer. Hand him this letter, and bring me a signature for it.'

Bolitho nodded. 'I see, sir.'

'I doubt it, but no matter, so off you go.'

Bolitho looked at the address scrawled on the wax-sealed envelope and then returned to the deck.

He led Dancer to the side and said, 'If I'm not back aboard before you leave, good luck, Martyn.' He touched his arm and smiled, surprised at his sudden uneasiness. 'And take care.'

Then he climbed on to the jetty and strode quickly towards the town.

It took over an hour to find the revenue officer in question. He seemed out of sorts, probably because of the extra work he was being given, and also at having to sign for the letter, as if he was not to be trusted.

When Bolitho returned to the jetty nothing seemed to have changed. Not at first glance. But as he drew nearer to the *Avenger*'s tall mast and furled sails he realized that the waggons had already gone.

As he lowered himself to the deck Truscott, the gunner, said, 'You're wanted below, sir.'

Again? It never stopped. He was still a midshipman, no matter what title Hugh had chosen for him.

Hugh Bolitho was seated at the table, as if he had not moved. The air was still wreathed in smoke, and it gave the impression that Whiffin had only just left.

'You didn't take long, Richard.' He sounded preoccupied. 'Good. You can tell Mr Gloag to call the hands and prepare to get under way. We'll be short-handed, so see that they know what they are doing.'

'The waggons are gone.'

His brother watched him for several seconds. 'Yes. Soon after you left.' He raised one eyebrow. 'Well?'

'Is something wrong?' Bolitho stood his ground as he recognized the quick flash of impatience.

'Whiffin brought news. There is to be an ambush. The waggons will take the road to the east'rd towards Helston, then nor'-east to Truro. Whiffin has made good use of his time ashore and a few guineas in the right palms. If all goes as expected, the attack will be between here and Helston. The coast road is within easy reach of a dozen coves and beaches.

Avenger will get under way now and be ready and waiting to offer assistance.'

Bolitho waited for more. His brother was explaining crisply, confidently, but there was a difference. He sounded as if he was speaking his thoughts aloud to convince himself of something.

Bolitho said, 'And the letter I carried was for the dragoons?'

Hugh Bolitho leaned back against the curved timbers and said bitterly, 'There are no dragoons. They're not coming.'

Bolitho could not speak for several moments, seeing only his friend's face as they had parted, recalling Hugh's remark about *Avenger* being short-handed. The plan had been for ten seamen to go with *Dancer*, while the rest of the escort would be some revenue officers. The dragoons from Truro, superbly trained and experienced, were to have been the main force.

The fact that Hugh had sent more seamen than intended showed he had known for some while.

He said, 'You knew. Just as you did about the informant Portlock.'

'Yes. If I had told you, what would you have done, eh?' He looked away. 'You'd have passed the news to Mr Dancer, frightened him half to death before he'd even started.'

'As it is, you might be sending him to his death.'

'Don't be so bloody insolent!' Hugh stood up, stooping automatically between the deckhead beams. It made him look as if he was about to spring at his younger brother. 'Or so self-righteous!'

'I could ride after them.' He could hear his own voice. Pleading, knowing at the same time it was wasted. 'There'll be other ways of catching the smugglers, other times.'

'It is settled. We sail on the tide. The wind has veered and is in our favour.' Hugh lowered his voice. 'Rest easy. We'll manage.'

As Bolitho made for the door he added, 'Mr Dancer is your friend, and we are brothers. But to all else we are authority, with a plain duty to carry out.' He nodded. 'So be about it, eh?'

Standing aft by the taffrail as he watched the *Avenger*'s depleted company preparing to take in the mooring lines, Bolitho tried to see it as his brother had suggested. Detached. Uninvolved. It would be simple to recall the waggons. A fast horse would be up to them in less than two hours. But Hugh was not prepared to risk his plan, no matter what chance it had of success without the dragoons' aid. He would rather put Dancer and two dozen of his own men in mortal danger.

Standing out of harbour almost into the eye of the wind, the *Avenger* made a leisurely exit.

Bolitho watched his brother by the compass, seeking some sign, a hint of his true feelings.

He heard Gloag say, 'Damn this fair weather, I say, sir. We'll not be able to change tack 'til we're hid from the land by dusk.' He sounded anxious, which was unusual. 'Time's runnin' out.'

Then Bolitho saw through his brother's guard as he thrust himself away from the compass with a sharp retort. 'Keep your miseries to yourself, Mr Gloag! I'm in no mood for them!'

He went below, and Bolitho heard the cabin door slam shut.

The acting-master remarked to the deck at large, 'Squalls ahead.'

Darkness had closed over the choppy waters of Mounts Bay when Hugh Bolitho came on deck again.

He nodded to Gloag and the watchkeepers on the lee side and said, 'Tell Mr Pyke and the gunner to attend to both boats. They must be armed and ready for hoisting outboard at short notice.' He peered at the feeble compass light. 'Call the hands and bring her about. Steer due east, if you please.'

As the word was passed between decks, and the seamen came hurrying once more to their stations, he crossed to where Bolitho stood beside the helmsmen.

'It'll be a clear night. Wind's brisk, but no need to take in a reef.'

Bolitho barely heard him. He was picturing the cutter's progress, as if he were a sea-bird high overhead.

From the calculations on the chart, and the new course, he knew that they would be heading inshore again, to dangerous shoal waters, towards the very coastline where the Dutchman had gone aground, and many more fine ships before.

If Whiffin's information was correct there would be an attack on the slow-moving waggons. If the attackers already knew of the deception they would be beside themselves with glee. If not, it would still make little difference unless Dancer and his men received help.

He looked up at the hard-bellied sails, the long whipping tongue of the masthead pendant.

His brother called, 'Very well. Stand by to come about.'

When order had replaced the confusion of changing tack, and *Avenger*'s long, pole-like bowsprit was pointing towards the east, the gunner came aft, leaning over to a steeper angle as the wind pushed the hull over.

'Boats checked an' ready, sir. An' I've got a good man by the arms chest in case we. . . .'

He swung round as a voice called hoarsely, 'Light, sir! On th' larboard bow!'

Dark figures slithered down across the tilting deck to the lee side to search for the light.

Someone said, 'Wreckers, mebbe?'

But Gloag, who had also seen it, said, 'No. It was too regular.' He pointed. 'See? There it be again!'

Bolitho snatched a telescope and tried to train it across the creaming wash of crests and spray. Two flashes. A shuttered lantern. A signal.

He felt Hugh at his side, heard his telescope squeak as he closed it and said, 'Where is that, d'you reckon, Mr Gloag?' Calm again. In charge.

''Ard t' tell, sir.'

Bolitho heard Gloag breathing heavily, any animosity between him and his youthful captain momentarily forgotten.

Pyke suggested, 'Round the point, towards Prah Sands, is my guess, sir.'

The light blinked out twice like a malevolent eye against the black shoreline.

Pyke said with disbelief, 'God damn their eyes, they're runnin' a cargo tonight, the buggers!'

Bolitho chilled, imagining the unknown vessel, somewhere ahead of the lightless cutter. If they sighted the *Avenger* they might sheer off. Then again, they might raise an alarm which in turn would warn the ambush. The attack would be brought forward and there would be no hope of quarter.

'We will shorten sail, Mr Gloag. Mr Truscott, have the guns loaded with grape and canister.' The sharpness in his tone held the gunner motionless. 'But do it piece by piece. I don't want to hear a sound!' Hugh peered round for a boatswain's mate. 'Pass the word forrard. A flogging for the first man to alert the enemy. A golden guinea for the first man to sight him!'

Bolitho crossed the deck before he knew what he was doing.

'You're not going after her?'

His brother faced him, although his face was hidden in the gloom.

'What did you expect? If I let her slip away we could lose both. This way we might do for all the devils at once!'

He swung away as the hands ran to the braces and halliards.

'I've no choice.'

7

A Tragedy

As the *Avenger* ploughed her way through each succession of wave crests, Bolitho found it harder to contain his anxiety. The cutter seemed to be making an incredible noise, and although he knew it would not be heard beyond half a cable, he could find no comfort. The sluice of water against the hull, the boom of heavy canvas with the attendant strains and rattles in the rigging, all joined in an ever-changing crescendo.

The topsail had been taken in, as had the jib, but even under fore and mainsail alone *Avenger* would stand out to any watchful smuggler.

As Gloag had mentioned, it was a fair night. Now that their eyes had become accustomed to it, it seemed even brighter. No clouds, a million glittering stars to reflect on the frothing waves and spume, and when you looked up the sails were like great, quivering wings.

A man craned over a stocky six-pounder and thrust out his arm.

'There, sir! Fine on th' lee bow!'

Figures moved about the decks, as if taking part in a well practised dance. Here and there a telescope squeaked or a man whispered to his companion. Some in speculation, others probably in envy for the man who would receive a golden guinea.

Hugh Bolitho said, 'Schooner, showing no lights. Under full sail too.' He shut his glass with a snap. 'Bit of luck. He'll be making more din than we are.' He dispensed with conjecture and added shortly, 'Bring her up a point, Mr Gloag. I don't want the devil to slip past us. We'll hold the wind-gage if we can.'

Voices passed hushed orders, and cordage squeaked through the sheaves while overhead the big mainsail shivered violently before filling again to the alteration of course.

Bolitho glanced at the compass as the helmsman said hoarsely, 'East by south, sir.'

'Man the larboard battery.' Hugh sounded completely absorbed. 'Open the ports.'

Bolitho watched the port lids being hauled open to reveal the glistening mane of water alongside. *Avenger* was heeling so far over that spray came leaping inboard over the six-pounders and deadly looking swivels.

Normally Bolitho would have felt like the rest of the men around him. Tense, committed, slightly wild at the prospect of a fight. But he could not lose himself this time, and kept thinking of the waggons, the outnumbered escort, the sudden horror of an ambush.

A light spurted in the darkness, and for an instant
he thought some careless seaman had dropped a
lantern on the other vessel. Then he heard a distant
crack, like a man breaking a nut in his palms, and
knew it was a pistol shot. A warning, a signal. Now
it did not matter which.

'Put up your helm, Mr Gloag!' Hugh's voice, loud
now that caution was pointless, made the men at the
tiller start. 'Stand by on deck!'

There were more flashes, doing more to reveal the
other vessel's size and sail plan than to harm the
crouching seamen.

The distance was rapidly falling away, the big
sails sweeping the cutter downwind like a bird of
prey, and then they saw the schooner rising through
the darkness, her canvas in confusion as she tried to
change tack and beat clear.

Bolitho watched his brother as he stood by the
weather rail, one foot on a bollard, as if he was watching a race.

'As you bear, Mr Truscott! On the uproll!'

A further pause, and across the choppy water
Bolitho heard muffled shouts, a vague rasp of metal.
Then, '*Fire!*'

At a range of less than seventy yards the larboard
battery hurled themselves inboard on their tackles,
their long orange tongues as blinding as their explosions were deafening. Unlike the heavy artillery
of a ship of the line, or even a frigate, *Avenger*'s little
six-pounders had voices which scraped the insides of
the brain.

Bolitho pictured the effect of the sweeping hail of

grape and close-packed canister as it cut into the other vessel's deck. He heard a spar fall, saw splashes alongside the darkened schooner as rigging and perhaps men dropped from the masts like dead fruit.

'Sponge out! Load!'

Hugh Bolitho had drawn his sword, and in the misty starlight it shone in his hand like a piece of thin ice. The same one he had used to settle a matter of honour. Probably many others too, Bolitho thought despairingly.

'*Fire!*'

Even as the small broadside crashed out again, shaking the hull like a giant fist, a few cracks and flashes showed that the smugglers were not ready to surrender.

Hugh Bolitho yelled, 'Stand by to board!' He did not even look round as a man fell kicking on the deck with a musket ball in his neck.

How many times they must have drilled and practised this, Bolitho thought as he dragged out his hanger. The gun crews left their smoking charges and seized up cutlasses and pikes, axes and dirks, while the remainder of the hands threw themselves on sheets and halliards. At the moment of collision between the two hulls, *Avenger*'s sails seemed to vanish like magic, so that with the way off her heavy, downwind plunge she came alongside the other vessel with one heart-stopping lurch.

But stripping off her sails had lessened the chance of dismasting her, likewise she did not rebound away from her adversary, so that as grapnels soared through the darkness and more shots and cries echoed between

the hulls, the first boarders swarmed across the bulwark.

Pyke yelled, 'Back, lads!'

Even that was like part of a rehearsed dance. As
the cheering boarders threw themselves inboard
again, two swivels exploded from the forecastle,
scything through a crowd of screaming figures who
seconds earlier had been rushing to repel the attack.

Hugh Bolitho pointed his sword. '*Now!* At 'em,
lads!' Then he was up and over, slashing at a man as
he did so, and catching one of his own as he all but
fell between the two grinding hulls.

Bolitho ran to the forecastle, waving his hanger to
the last party of boarders.

Yelling and cheering like demons they clambered
over the gap. One man fell beside Bolitho without a
sound, another threw his hand to his face and screamed, the sound ending with a sharp gasp as a boarding
pike came out of the darkness and impaled him.

Shoulder to shoulder Bolitho's men advanced
along the schooner's deck, while from the cutter
alongside the remaining seamen yelled advice and
warnings, accompanied by pistol-fire and a few well
aimed missiles.

Bolitho felt his shoes slithering on the remains left
by the swivels' murderous onslaught. He shut his
mind to all else but the faces which loomed and
faded before him, the jarring ache of steel as he kept
up his guard and probed for weakness in an oppon-
ent's defence.

Across the heads and shoulders of the yelling,
cursing men he saw his brother's white lapels, heard

his voice as he urged his party forward, separating and dividing the defenders into smaller and smaller groups.

Someone yelled, '*That's* for Jackie Trillo, you bugger!' A cutlass swung like a scythe, almost cutting a man's head from his shoulders.

'Strike! Throw down your arms!'

But a few more were to fall before the cutlasses and pikes clattered on the planking amongst the corpses and groaning wounded.

Then Bolitho saw his brother point his sword at a man by the untended wheel.

'Have your people anchor. If you desist or try to scuttle, I will have you seized up and flogged.' He sheathed his sword. 'Then hanged.'

Bolitho hurried to his side. 'The whole of Cornwall will have heard this!'

Hugh did not seem to be listening. 'Not Frenchies as I suspected. They sound like Colonists.' He turned abruptly and nodded. 'Yes, I agree. We will leave the prize anchored here, under guard. Have two swivels hoisted across and trained on the prisoners. Then put a petty officer in charge. He'll know how to deal with them. He'd rather die than face me after letting them escape!'

Bolitho followed him, his mind awhirl as he watched his brother's progress. Passing orders, answering questions, his hands moving to emphasize a point or to indicate what he wanted done.

Pyke shouted, 'Anchor's down, sir!'

'Good.' Hugh Bolitho strode to the side. 'The rest of you, come with me. Mr Gloag! Cast off and get the ship under way, if you please!'

Blocks squeaked, and like rearing spectres the sails rose above the listing, pock-marked schooner. Reluctantly at first, and then with gathering speed, the *Avenger* jerked and bumped her way free of the other vessel's side, the sails filling immediately to carry her clear.

'Where to, sir?' Gloag was peering at the sails. 'It's a mite more dangerous 'ere.'

'Put a good leadsman in the chains, please. Sounding all the way. We'll anchor in four fathoms and sway out the boats.' He looked at his brother. 'We'll head inland in two groups and cut the road.'

'Aye, aye, sir.'

Surprisingly, Hugh clapped him on the arm. 'Cheer up, man! A fine prize, full of smuggled booty, I shouldn't wonder, and no more than a few men killed! We can only take one step at a time!'

As the cutter groped her way closer and closer to the land, the leadsman's dreary chant recorded the growing danger. Eventually, with surf to starboard, and a dark hint of land beyond, they dropped anchor. But for Gloag's anxiety and repeated warnings, Bolitho suspected his brother would have gone even nearer.

Even now, he did not envy Gloag's responsibility. Anchored amidst sand-bars and jagged rocks, without sufficient hands to work her clear if the wind rose again, he would be hard put to stop *Avenger* dragging and being pushed ashore.

If Hugh Bolitho was also conscious of it he concealed his fears well.

The two boats were lowered, and taking all but a

handful of men, they headed for the nearest beach. The boats were filled to the gunwales, and each man was armed to the teeth.

But as the oars rose and fell, and the land thrust out to enfold them, Bolitho could feel the emptiness. The sounds of gunfire would have been enough. The people who had been making the signals, and any others involved, would be in their cottages by now, or galloping to some hiding-place as fast as they could manage.

Once assembled on the small beach, with the sea pushing and then receding noisily through the rocks, Hugh said, 'We will divide here, Richard. I'll take the right side, you the left. Anybody who fails to stop when challenged will be fired on.' He nodded to his men. 'Lead on.'

In two long files the sailors started up the slope from the beach, at first expecting a shot or two, and then finally accepting that they were alone.

Bolitho crossed the narrow coast road, the wind whipping around his legs, as his men hurried out on either side. The waggons might be safe. Could already have passed on their way. There were certainly no wheel tracks to mark where the heavily loaded waggons had gone by.

The seaman named Robins held up his hand. '*Sir!*' Bolitho hurried to his side. 'Someone's comin'!'

The seamen scattered and vanished on either side of the rough track, and Bolitho heard the soft click of metal as they cocked their weapons in readiness.

Robins and Bolitho remained very still beside a wind-twisted bush.

The seaman said softly, 'Just th' one, sir. Drunk, by th' sound of it.' He grinned. 'Not been as busy as th' rest of us!' His grin froze as they heard a man sobbing and gasping with pain.

Then they saw him reeling back and forth across the road, almost falling in his pitiful efforts to hurry. No wonder Robins had thought him drunk.

Robins exclaimed, 'Oh God, sir! It's one of our lads! It's Billy Snow!'

Before Bolitho could stop him he ran towards the lurching figure and caught him in his arms.

'What is it, Billy?'

The man swayed and gasped, 'Where was you, Tom? Where *was* you?'

Bolitho and some of the others helped Robins to lay the man down. How he had got this far was a miracle. He was cut and bleeding from several wounds and his clothing was sodden with blood.

As they tried to cover his injuries, Snow said in a small voice, 'We was doin' very well, sir, an' then we sees the soldiers, comin' down the road like a cavalry charge!'

He whimpered, and someone said harshly, 'Easy with that wound, Tom!'

Snow muttered vaguely, 'Some of the lads gave a huzza, just for a joke, like, an' young Mr Dancer went on ahead to greet them.'

Bolitho stooped lower, feeling the man's despair, the nearness of death.

'Then, an' then. . . .'

Bolitho touched his shoulder. 'Easy now. Take your time.'

'Aye, sir.' In the strange star-glow his face looked like wax, and his eyes were tightly shut. He tried again. 'They rode straight amongst us, hackin' an' slashin', not givin' us a chance. It was all done in a minute.'

He coughed, and Robins whispered huskily, ' 'E's goin', sir.'

Bolitho asked, 'What about the others?'

The head jerked painfully. Like a puppet's. 'Back there. Up th' road. All dead, I think, though some ran towards the sea.'

Bolitho turned away, his eyes smarting. Sailors would run towards the sea. Feeling betrayed and lost, it was all they knew.

' 'E's dead, sir.'

They all stood round looking at the dead man. Where had he been going? What had he hoped to do in his last moments?

'The cap'n's comin', sir.'

Hugh Bolitho, with his men at his back, came out of the darkness, so that the road seemed suddenly crowded. They all looked at the corpse.

'So we were too late.' Hugh Bolitho bent over the dead man. 'Snow. A good hand.' He straightened up and added abruptly, 'Better get it over with.' He walked down the middle of the road, straight-backed. Completely alone.

It did not take long to find the others. They were scattered over the road, the rocky slope beyond, or apparently hurled bodily over the edge on to the hillside.

There was blood everywhere, and as the seamen

lit their lanterns the dead eyes lit up in the gloom as if to follow their efforts, to curse them for their betrayal.

The waggons and the escort's own weapons had all gone. Not all the men were there who should have been, and Bolitho guessed they had either fled into the darkness or been taken prisoners for some terrible reason. And this was Cornwall. His own home. No more than fifteen miles from Falmouth. On this wild coastline it could just as easily have been a hundred.

A man Bolitho recognized as Mumford, a boat-swain's mate came from the roadside. He held out a cocked hat and said awkwardly, 'I think this is Mr Dancer's, sir.'

Bolitho took it and felt it. It was cold and wet.

A cry brought more men running as a wounded seaman was found hiding in a fold of rocks above the road.

Bolitho went to see if he could help and then stopped, frozen in his tracks. As Robins held up his lantern to assist the others with the wounded and barely conscious man, he saw something pale through the wet grass.

Robins said fiercely, ' 'Ere, sir, I'll look.'

They clambered up the slippery grass together, the lantern's beam shining feebly on a sprawled body. It was the fair hair Bolitho had seen, but now that he was nearer he could see the blood mingling with it as well.

'Stay here.'

He took the lantern and ran the rest of the way. Gripping the blue coat he turned the body over, so that the dead eyes seemed to stare at him with sudden anger.

He released his grip, ashamed of his relief. It was not Dancer, but a dead revenue man, cut down as he had tried to escape the slaughter.

He heard Robins ask, 'All right, sir?'

He controlled the nausea and nodded. 'Give me a hand with this poor fellow.'

Hours later, dispirited and worn out, they reassembled on the beach in the first grey light of dawn.

Seven more survivors had been found, or had emerged from various hiding places at the sound of their voices. Martyn Dancer was not one of them.

As he climbed aboard the cutter Gloag said gruffly, 'If 'e's alive, then there's 'ope, Mr Bolitho.'

Bolitho watched the jolly boat pulling ashore again, Peploe, the sailmaker, and his mate sitting grimly in the sternsheets, going to sew up the corpses for burial.

There would be hell to pay for this night's work, Bolitho thought wretchedly. He thought of the fair-headed corpse, the sick despair giving way to hope as he realized it was not his friend.

But now as he watched the bleak shoreline, the small figures on the beach, he felt there was not much hope either.

8

Voice in the Dark

Harriet Bolitho entered the room, her velvet gown noiseless against the door. For a few seconds she stood watching her son silhouetted against the fire, his hands outstretched towards the flames. Nearby, her youngest daughter Nancy sat on a rug, her knees drawn up to her chin as she watched him, as if willing him to speak.

Through another set of double doors she could hear the rumble of voices, blurred and indistinct. They had been in the old library for over an hour. Sir Henry Vyvyan, Colonel de Crespigny of the dragoons, and of course Hugh.

As was often the case, the news of the ambush and the capture of a suspected smuggler had reached Falmouth overland long before the *Avenger* and her prize had anchored in the Roads.

She had been expecting something to happen, to go wrong. Hugh had always been headstrong, unwilling to take advice. His command, no matter how junior, had been the worst thing which could have happened. He needed a firm hand, like Richard's captain.

She straightened her back and crossed the room, smiling for him. They needed their father here and now more than anyone.

Richard looked up at her, his face lined with strain.

'How long will they be?'

She shrugged. 'The colonel has tried to explain why his men were not on the road. They were ordered to Bodmin at the last moment. Something to do with bullion being moved across the country. De Crespigny is making a full inquiry, and our squire has been sent for too.'

Bolitho looked at his hands. He was only feet from the fire but was still cold. His brother's hornets' nest was here, amongst them.

Like the dazed and bewildered survivors of the ambush, he had found himself hating the dragoons for not riding to their aid. But he had had time to think about it, and could see the colonel's dilemma. An unlikely scheme to catch some smugglers set against his rigid orders for escorting a fortune in gold was barely worth considering. He would also have assumed that Hugh would call off the attempt once he had been told about the change of circumstances.

He blurted out, 'But what will they do about Martyn?'

She stood behind him and touched his hair.

'All they can, Richard. Poor boy, I keep thinking of him too.'

The library doors opened and the three men entered the room.

What an ill-assorted trio, Bolitho thought. His brother, tight-lipped, and shabby in his sea-going uniform. Vyvyan, massive and grim, his terrible scar adding to his appearance of strength, and the dragoons' colonel, as neat and as elegant as a King's guard. It was hard to believe he had ridden many miles without dismounting.

Harriet Bolitho's chin lifted. 'Well, Sir Henry? What do *you* think about it?'

Vyvyan rubbed his chin. 'I believe, ma'am, that these devils have taken young Dancer as hostage, so to speak. What for, I can't guess, but it looks bad, and we must face up to it.'

De Crespigny said, 'Had I more men, another two troops of horses at least, I might do more, but. . . .' He did not finish.

Bolitho watched them wearily. Each was protecting himself. Getting ready to lay the blame elsewhere when the real authorities heard what had happened. He looked at his brother. There was no doubt whose head would be on the block this time.

Nancy whispered, 'I shall pray for him, Dick.'

He looked at her and smiled. She was holding Martyn's hat, drying it by the fire. Keeping it like a talisman.

Vyvyan continued, 'It's no use acceptin' defeat. We'll have to put our ideas together.'

Voices murmured in the hallway, and moments later Mrs Tremayne peered into the room. Behind her Bolitho could see Pendrith, the gamekeeper, hovering with obvious impatience.

His mother asked, 'What is it, Pendrith?'

Pendrith came into the room, smelling of damp and earth. He knuckled his forehead to the standing figures and nodded to Nancy.

He said in his harsh voice, 'One of the colonel's men is outside with a message, ma'am.' As the colonel made his excuses and bustled outside, Pendrith added quickly, 'An' I've got this, sir.' He thrust out his fist with a small roll of paper for Vyvyan to read.

Vyvyan's solitary eye scanned the crude handwriting and he exclaimed, '*To whom it may concern*. . . . what the hell?' The eye moved more quickly and he said suddenly, 'It's a demand. As I thought. They've taken young Dancer as hostage.'

Bolitho asked, 'For what?' His heart was beating painfully and he could barely breathe.

Vyvyan handed the letter to Mrs Bolitho and said heavily, 'The one wrecker that my men were able to capture. They want to exchange Dancer for him. Otherwise. . . .' He looked away.

Hugh Bolitho stared at him. 'Even if we were allowed to bargain. . . .' He got no further.

Vyvyan swung round, his shadow filling the room. '*Allowed?* What are you sayin', man? This is a life at stake. If we hang that rascal in chains at some crossroads gibbet they will kill young Dancer, and we all know it. They may do so anyway, but I think they will keep their word. A revenue man is one thing, a King's officer another.'

Hugh Bolitho met his gaze, his face stiff with resentment.

'He was doing his duty.'

Vyvyan took a few paces from the fire. He sounded impatient, exasperated.

'See it this way. We know the wrecker's identity. We may well catch him again, when there'll be no escape from the hangman. But Dancer's life is valuable, to his family and to his country.' He hardened his tone. 'Besides which, it will look better.'

'I don't see that, sir.'

Hugh Bolitho was pale with tiredness but showed no sign of weakening.

'You don't, eh? Then let me explain it for you. How will it sound at a court of enquiry later on? A midshipman's loss is bad enough, the deaths of all those sailors and revenue officers hard to explain, let alone those damned muskets which are now in the wrong hands. But who got clean away without hurt? The *Avenger*'s two officers, *both of this family*!'

For the first time Hugh Bolitho looked shocked.

'That was not how it was, sir. But for the schooner, we would have been well placed to assist, dragoons or no dragoons.'

The colonel entered at that moment and said quietly, 'I have just had word that the schooner's crew are ashore and under close guard. They will be taken to Truro.'

Vyvyan handed him the crumpled letter and watched his face.

The colonel said savagely, 'I guessed it would not end there, damn them!'

Hugh Bolitho persisted stubbornly, 'That schooner was carrying gold coin by the box-load. The crew are all American Colonists. I have no doubt they

intended to use the money to buy muskets, here in
Cornwall. Then they would likely transfer them to a
larger vessel at some safe rendezvous elsewhere.'

The colonel eyed him coldly. 'The schooner's
master insists he is innocent. That he was lost, and
that you fired on him without warning. He took you
for a pirate.' He raised one hand wearily. 'I *know*,
Mr Bolitho, but it is what everyone will believe who
wants to. You lost your muskets, failed to capture
any of the smugglers, and several men have died for
no good reason. I know there is talk of unrest in the
American Colony, but it is only talk at present. What
you have done is very real.'

Vyvyan said gruffly, 'Be easy on him. We were all
youngsters once. I told him we should agree to
exchange our prisoners. After all, we have a good
prize in the harbour, if the magistrates can prove she
was after the guns. And when we get Dancer back safe
and sound he might tell us more.' He gave a crooked
smile. 'What say you, Colonel?'

De Crespigny sighed. 'It is no matter for a land-
owner or a young lieutenant to dabble with. Even I
will need to be directed in this case.' He looked
round to make certain that the gamekeeper had
gone. 'However, if your captured felon should
escape, I see no reason to report it just yet, eh?'

Vyvyan grinned. 'Spoken like a true soldier! Well
done. I'll have my men deal with it.' His eye moved
across the Bolitho family. 'But if I am wrong, and
they harm young Dancer, they will eventually be
very sorry for what they have done.'

Hugh Bolitho nodded. 'Very well. I accept the

plan, sir. But after this I will stand no chance of success in these waters. My command and all in her will be laughed into oblivion.'

Bolitho looked at his brother and felt sorry for him. But there was no other way.

The others eventually left the house and Hugh said vehemently, 'If I could have laid hands on just one of them. I'd have finished this damned affair once and for all!'

The next two days were filled with suspense and anxiety at the Bolitho house. There was silence from Dancer's captors, although no further proof was needed as to the value of the letter. Some gilt buttons, cut from a midshipman's coat, and a neckcloth which Bolitho recognized as Dancer's were found outside the gates as a blunt warning.

On the second night the two brothers were alone by the fire, each unwilling to break the silence.

Then Hugh said suddenly, 'I shall go down to the *Avenger*. You had better remain here until we hear something. One way or the other.'

Bolitho asked, 'After this, what will you do?'

'Do?' He laughed. 'Go back to some damned ship as a junior lieutenant, I expect. Promotion went through the window when I failed to finish what I came to do.'

Bolitho stood up as horses clattered in the yard. A door banged open and he saw Mrs Tremayne staring at him, her eyes filling her face.

'They've got him, Master Richard! They've *found* him!'

In the next instant the room seemed to be full.

Servants, some troopers and Pendrith, the game-keeper, who said, 'The soldiers discovered 'im walkin' along the road, sir. 'Is 'ands were tied behind 'is back and 'e was blindfolded. Wonder 'e didn't go 'ead-first off the cliff!'

They all fell silent as Dancer, covered from head to foot in a long cloak, came into the room, supported on either side by two of de Crespigny's dragoons.

Bolitho strode forward and gripped his shoulders. He could barely speak, and they looked at each other for several more seconds until Dancer said simply, 'Near thing that time, Dick.'

Harriet Bolitho pushed through the watching figures and lifted the cloak from Dancer's shoulders. Then she took him in her arms, pulling his head to her shoulder, tears running unheeded down her cheeks.

'Oh, you poor boy!'

Dancer's captors had stripped him of all but his breeches. Blindfolded and stumbling barefoot along a road unknown to him, had he fallen, he would certainly have died of the bitter cold. Someone had beaten him too, and Bolitho saw weals on his back like rope burns.

Mrs Bolitho said huskily, 'Mrs Tremayne, take these good men to the kitchen. Give them anything they want, money too.'

The soldiers beamed and shuffled their boots. 'Thankee, ma'am. It was a real pleasure to be sure.'

Dancer lowered himself in front of the fire and said quietly, 'I was carried to a small village. I heard someone say it was supposed to be a witches' place.

That nobody would dare come looking for me there.
They laughed about it. Told me how they were going
to kill me if you didn't release their man.'

He looked up at Hugh Bolitho. 'I am sorry I failed
you, sir. But our attackers looked like real soldiers,
and acted without mercy.' He shuddered and touched
his arm as if to hide his nakedness.

Hugh replied, 'What's done is done, Mr Dancer.
But I'm glad you are safe. I mean it.'

Mrs Bolitho brought a cup of hot soup. 'Drink
this, Martyn. Then bed.' She sounded composed
again.

Dancer looked at Bolitho. 'I was blindfolded all
the time. When I tried to get it off I felt them holding
a hot iron close to my face. One of them said that if
I did it again I would not need a blindfold. The iron
would take care of my sight.'

He shivered as Nancy covered his shoulders with a
woollen shawl.

Hugh Bolitho banged his fist against the wall.
'They were clever. They knew you'd not recognize
their faces, but thought you might recall where you
were being held!'

Dancer got painfully to his feet and grimaced. He
had cut them badly along the way before the troopers
had found him.

'I know one of them.'

They all stared at him, thinking he was about to
break down.

Dancer looked at Mrs Bolitho and held out his
hands until she took them in hers.

'It was the first day. I was lying in the darkness,

waiting to die, when I heard him. I don't think they'd told him I was there.' He tightened his grip on her hands. 'It was the man I saw here, ma'am. The one called Vyvyan.'

She nodded slowly, her face full of sympathy.

'You've suffered enough, Martyn, and we have been very worried for you.' She kissed him gently on the lips. 'Now to bed with you. You'll find everything you need.'

Hugh Bolitho was still staring at him as if he had misheard.

'Sir Henry? Are you *certain*?'

She exclaimed, 'Leave it, Hugh! There's been harm enough done to this boy!'

Bolitho watched his brother's strength returning, like a sudden squall approaching a becalmed ship.

'A boy to you, Mother. But he is still one of my officers.' Hugh could barely conceal his excitement. 'Right here under our noses. No wonder Vyvyan's men were always nearby and we never caught anyone. He had to rid himself of his so-called prisoner before an examining judge arrived. The man would have informed on him to save his own life.'

Bolitho felt his mouth go dry. Vyvyan had even had some of his own men shot down to make it look perfect. He was a monster, not a man at all. And it had nearly worked, might still work if Dancer's story was not believed.

Wrecker, smuggler and an important part of some planned uprising in America, it was like a growing nightmare.

Vyvyan had planned all of it, outwitted the

authorities from the very beginning. He had even put the idea of exchanging hostages in their minds.

To his brother Bolitho said, 'What will you do?'

He gave him a bitter smile. 'I am inclined to send word to the admiral. But now we will try to determine where this village is. It cannot be far from the sea.' His eyes shone like fires. 'Next time, Richard, *next* time he will be less fortunate!'

Bolitho followed Dancer up the stairs, past the watching portraits and into his room.

'In future, Martyn, I will never complain about serving in a ship of the line.'

Dancer sat on the edge of the bed and cocked his head to listen to the wind against a window.

'Nor I.' He rolled over, worn out with exhaustion.

As his head lay in the glow of some candles, Bolitho thought of that other one, dead in the wet grass, and was suddenly grateful.

9

The Devil's Hand

Colonel de Crespigny sat stiffly in the *Avenger*'s stern
cabin looking around with a mixture of curiosity and
distaste.

He said, 'As I have just explained to your, er
captain, I cannot take a risk on such meagre evidence.'

As both the midshipmen made to protest he added
hastily, 'I am not saying I disbelieve what you heard
or what you *thought* you heard. But in a court of law
and make no mistake, a man in Sir Henry's position
and authority would go to the highest advocates, i
would sound less than convincing.'

He leaned towards Dancer, his polished boots
creaking on the deck.

'Think of it yourself. A good advocate from London
an experienced assize judge and a biased jury, your
word would be the only voice of protest. The
schooner's crew can be held upon suspicion, although
there is nothing so far to connect them with Sir
Henry or any evil purpose. I am certain that fresh

evidence will come to hand, but against them, and
not the man we are after.'

Hugh Bolitho lay with his shoulders against the
cutter's side, his eyes half closed as he said, 'It seems
we are in irons.'

The colonel picked up a goblet and filled it carefully before saying, 'If you can discover the village,
and some good, strong evidence, then you will have a
case. Otherwise you may have to rely on Sir Henry's
support at any court of enquiry. Cruel and unjust it
may be, but you must think of yourselves now.'

Bolitho watched his brother, sharing his sense of
defeat and injustice. If Vyvyan was to suspect what
they were doing, he might already have put some
further plan into motion to disgrace or implicate them.

Gloag, who had been invited to the little meeting
because of his experience if not for his authority,
said gruffly, 'There be a 'undred such villages an'
'amlets within five miles of us, sir. It might take
months.'

Hugh Bolitho said harshly, 'By which time the
word will have penetrated the admiral's ear and
Avenger will have been sent elsewhere, no doubt with
a new commander!'

De Crespigny nodded. 'Likely so. I have served in
the Army for a long while and I am still surprised by
the ways of my superiors.'

Hugh Bolitho reached for a goblet and then
changed his mind.

'I have made my written report for the admiral,
and to the senior officer of Customs and Excise at
Penzance. Whiffin, my clerk-in-charge, is making

the copies now. I have sent word to the relatives o
the dead and arranged for the sale of their belonging
within the vessel.' He spread his hands. 'I feel at
loss as to what else to do.'

Bolitho looked at him closely, seeing him as a fa
different person from the confident, sometime
arrogant brother he had come to expect.

He said, 'We must find the village. Before the
move the muskets and any other booty they've seize
by robbing or wrecking. There must be a clue. Ther
has to be.'

De Crespigny sighed. 'I agree. But if I send ever
man and horse under my command, I'd discove
nothing. The thieves would go to earth like foxe
and Sir Henry would guess we were on to him. Bu
"capturing" that wrecker and then exchanging hir
was a master-stroke. It would convince any jury, le
alone a Cornish one.'

Dancer exclaimed, 'Sir Henry Vyvyan told you h
knew the prisoner and would catch up with him on
day.'

De Crespigny shook his head. 'If you are righ
about Sir Henry, he will have killed that man, o
sent him far away where he can do no harm.'

But Hugh Bolitho snapped, 'No, Mr Dancer ha
made the only sort of sense I have heard today.' H
looked about the cabin as if to escape. 'Vyvyan is too
clever, too shrewd to falsify something which coul
be checked. If we can find out who the man was, and
where he came from, we may be on our way to suc
cess!' He seemed to come alive again. 'It is all w
have, for God's sake!'

Gloag nodded with approval. ' 'E'll be from one of
ir 'Enry's farms, I'll bet odds on it.'

Bolitho could feel the flicker of hope moving around
he cabin, frail, but better than a minute earlier.

He said, 'We'll send to the house. Ask Hardy. He
used to work for Vyvyan before he came to us.'

De Crespigny stared. 'Your head gardener? I'd
need a higher trust than that if I had so much in the
balance!'

Hugh Bolitho smiled. 'But with respect, sir, you do
not. It is my career in the scales, and the good name
of my family.'

Avenger rolled lazily at her cable, as if she too was
eager to be at sea again, to play her part.

Bolitho asked, 'Well? Shall we try?'

Bill Hardy was an old man whose touch with his
plants and flowers was better than his fading eye-
sight. But he had lived all his life within ten square
miles and knew a great deal about everyone. He kept
to himself, and Bolitho suspected that his father had
taken him on because he was sorry for him, or
because Vyvyan had never tried to hide his admir-
ation for and interest in Mrs Bolitho.

Hugh Bolitho said, 'As soon as we can. Carefully
though. An alarm now would be a disaster.'

Surprisingly, he allowed his brother and Dancer to
return to the house with the mission. To keep it as
simple as possible, or to avoid the risk of losing his
temper, Bolitho was unsure.

As they hurried across the cobbled square Dancer
said breathlessly, 'I am beginning to feel free again!
Whatever happens next, I think I am ready for it!'

Bolitho looked at him and smiled. They had been looking forward to Christmas together and facing one of Mrs Tremayne's fantastic dinners. But the immediate future, like the grey weather and hint of rain, was less encouraging than it had seemed in *Avenger*'s cabin. It seemed likely they would be facing the table of a court of enquiry rather than Mr Tremayne's.

Bolitho found his mother in the library writing a letter. One of the many to her husband. There must be a dozen or more at sea at any one time, he thought. Or lying under the seal of some port admiral awaiting his ship's arrival.

She listened to their idea and offered without hesitation. 'I will speak with him.'

'Hugh said no.' Bolitho protested, 'None of us want you implicated.'

She smiled. 'I became implicated when I met your father.' She threw a shawl over her head and added quietly, 'Old Hardy was to be transported to the colonies for stealing fish and food for his family. It had been a bad year, a poor harvest and much illness. In Falmouth alone we had some fifty people die of fever. Old Hardy lost his wife and child. His sacrifice, for he was a proud man, was for nothing.'

Bolitho nodded. Sir Henry Vyvyan could have saved him. But Hardy had made the additional mistake of stealing from him. It was another glimpse of his own father too. The stern, disciplined sea captain, who to please his wife had taken pity on the poor-sighted gardener and brought him here to Falmouth.

Dancer sat down and looked at the fire-place. 'She never fails to amaze me, Dick. I feel I know her better than my own mother!'

She returned within a quarter-hour and sat down at the desk again as if nothing had happened.

'The man's name is Blount, Arthur Blount. He has been in trouble before with the revenue men, but this is the first time he has been taken. He's never in honest work for long, and when he is it is of little value. In and around farms, repairing walls, digging ditches. Nothing for any length of time.'

Bolitho thought of the dead informant, Portlock. Like the man Blount, a scavenger, getting what he could, where he could.

She added, 'My advice is to return to your ship. I'll send word when I hear something.' She reached out and rested her hand on her son's shoulder, searching his face with her eyes as she said, 'But take care. Vyvyan is a very powerful man. Had it been anyone but Martyn here, I might have disbelieved he could do all these terrible things.' She smiled sadly at the fair-haired midshipman and said, 'But now that I know you, I am surprised I did not realize it for myself far earlier! He has links with the Americas and may well have further ambitions here. Force of arms? It is the way he has always lived, so why should he have changed now? It has taken a newcomer like Martyn to reveal him, that is all.'

The midshipmen made their way back to the anchored cutter, feeling the freshening edge to the wind, and noting that several of the smaller fishing

boats had already returned to the shelter of Carric
Roads.

Hugh Bolitho listened to their story, then said, '
have had a bellyful of waiting, but I can see no choic
this time.'

Later, when it was dark, and the anchorage aliv
with tossing white crests, Bolitho heard the watch o
deck challenge an approaching boat.

Dancer, who had been in charge of the anchor
watch, clattered down the ladder and struck hi
head against a deckhead beam without apparentl
noticing.

He said excitedly, 'It's your mother, Dick!' To th
cutter's commander he added in a more sober tone
'Mrs Bolitho, sir.'

She entered the cabin, her cloak and hair glisten
ing with blown spray. If anything it made her loo
younger than ever.

She said, 'Old Hardy knows the place, and s
should I! You remember the terrible fever I wa
telling you about? There was some wild talk that i
was a punishment for some witchcraft which wa
being performed in a tiny hamlet to the south of here
A mob dragged two poor women from their home
and burned them at the stake as witches. The wind
drunkenness, or just a mob getting out of hand
nobody really knew what happened, but the flame
from the two pyres spread to the cottages, and soor
the whole place was a furnace. When the military
arrived, it was all over. But most of the people who
lived in and around the hamlet believed it was powerful witchcraft which had destroyed their homes a

punishment for what they had done to two of their own.' She shivered. 'It is foolish of course, but simple folk live by simple laws.'

Hugh Bolitho let out a long breath. 'And Blount defied the beliefs and made his home there.' He looked at Dancer. 'And certain others shared his sanctuary, it seems.'

He stepped around his mother, shouting, 'Pass the word for my clerk!' To the others he said, 'I'll send a despatch to de Crespigny. We may need to search a big area.'

Dancer stared at him. 'Are *we* going?'

Hugh Bolitho smiled grimly. 'Aye. If it's another false lead, I need to know it before Vyvyan. And if it's true, I want to be in at the kill!' He lowered his voice and said to his mother, 'You should not have come yourself. You have done enough.'

Whiffin bowed through the door, staring at the woman as if he could not believe his eyes.

'A letter to the commandant at Truro, Whiffin. Then we will need horses and some good men who can ride as well as fight.'

'I have partly dealt with that, Hugh.' His mother watched his surprise with amusement. 'Horses, and three of our own men are on the jetty.'

Gloag said anxiously, 'Bless you, ma'am, I've not been in a saddle since I were a little lad.'

Hugh Bolitho was already buckling on his sword. 'You stay here. This is a young man's game.'

Within half an hour the party had assembled on the jetty. Three farm labourers, Hugh and his midshipmen, and six sailors who had sworn they could ide as well as any gentlemen. The latter included the resourceful Robins.

Hugh Bolitho faced them through a growing downpour.

'Keep together, men, and be ready.'

He turned as another rider galloped away into the darkness with the letter for Colonel de Crespigny.

'And if we meet the devils, I want no revenge killings, no *take this for cutting down our friends*. It is justice we need now.' He wheeled his mount on the wet stones. 'So be it!'

Once clear of the town the horses had to slow their pace because of the rain and the treacherous, deeply rutted road. But before long they were met by a solitary horseman, a long musket resting across his saddle like an ancient warrior.

'This way, Mr Hugh, sir.' It was Pendrith, the gamekeeper. 'I got wind of what you was about, sir.' He sounded as if he was grinning. 'Thought you might need a good forester.'

They hurried on in silence. Just the wet drumming of hoofs, the deep panting of horses and riders alike, with an occasional jingle of stirrup or cutlass.

Bolitho thought of his ride with Dancer, when they had joined the witless boy at the cove, with the corpse of Tom Morgan, the revenue man. Was it only weeks and days ago? It seemed like months.

As they drew nearer the burned out village Bolitho remembered something about it. How his mother had scolded him when as a small child he had borrowed a pony and gone there alone but for a dog.

This night she had described the superstition as foolish. Then, she had not sounded quite of the same mind.

The horses milled together as Pendrith dismounted and said, ' 'Alf a mile, sir, an' no more, at a guess. I think it best to go on foot.'

Hugh Bolitho jumped down. 'Tether the horses. Detail two men to stand guard.' He drew his pistol and wiped it free of rain with his sleeve. 'Lead on, Pendrith, I'm more used to the quarterdeck than chasing poachers!'

Bolitho noticed that some of the men chuckled at the remark. He was learning all the time.

Pendrith and one of the farm hands moved on ahead. There was no moon, but a diamond-shaped gap in the racing clouds gave a brief and eerie outline to a small, pointed roof.

Bolitho whispered to his friend, 'They still build these little witch houses in some villages here. To guard the entrances from evil.'

Dancer shifted uncomfortably in his borrowed clothing and hissed, 'They didn't have much success in this place, Dick!'

Pendrith's untidy shape came bounding amongst them, and Bolitho imagined he was being chased, or that some of the legends were true after all.

But the gamekeeper said urgently, 'There's a fire of sorts, sir! T'other side of the place!'

He turned, his face glowing red as a great tongue of flame soared skyward, the sparks whirling and carrying on the wind like a million spiteful fire-flies.

Several of the men cried out with fear, and even

Bolitho who was used to tales of local witches and their covens, felt ice running up his spine.

Hugh Bolitho charged through the bushes, all caution thrown aside as he yelled, 'They've fired a cottage! Lively, lads!'

When they reached the tiny cottage it was already blazing like an inferno. Great plumes of sparks swirled down amongst the smoke-blinded seamen, stinging them, trying to hold them at bay.

'Mr Dancer! Take two men and get around to the far side!'

In the fast spreading flames, the crouching seamen and farm hands stood out clearly against the back-cloth of trees and rain. Bolitho wrapped his neck-cloth around his mouth and nose and kicked at the sagging door with all his strength. More flames and sparks seared his legs, as with a rumbling crash the remains of the thatched roof and timbers collapsed within the cottage.

Pendrith was bawling, 'Come back, d'you hear, Master Richard! Ain't no use!'

Bolitho turned away and then saw his brother's face. He was staring at the flames, oblivious to the heat and the hissing sparks. In those few seconds it was all laid bare. His brother saw his own hopes and future burning with the cottage. Somebody had set it alight, no ordinary fire could burst out like this in the middle of a downpour. Equally quickly, he made up his mind.

He threw himself against the door again, shutting his mind to everything but the need to get inside.

It toppled before him like a charred draw-bridge,

and as the smoke billowed aside he saw a man's body twisting and kicking amongst burning furniture and black fragments of fallen thatch.

It all swept through his mind as he ran forward, stooping to grip the man's shoulders and drag him back towards the door. The man was kicking like a madman, and above a gag his eyes rolled with agony and terror. He was trussed hand and foot, and Bolitho was as sickened by the stench as by the act of leaving a man to burn alive.

Voices came and went through the roar of flames like the souls of dead witches returning for a final curse.

Then others were seizing his arms, taking the load and pulling them both out into the torrential, beautiful rain.

Dancer came running through the glare and shouted, 'It's the same place, Dick! I'm certain of it. The shape of the rear wall. . . .' He stopped to stare at the struggling, seared man on the ground.

Pendrith knelt down on the mud and embers and asked hoarsely, ' 'Oo done this thing to you?'

The man, whom Pendrith had already recognized as the missing Blount, gasped, 'They left me 'ere to burn!' He was writhing, his teeth bared in agony. 'They wouldn't listen to me!' He seemed to realize that there were sailors present and added brokenly, 'After all I done for 'im.'

Hugh bent over him, his face like stone as he asked, 'Who, man? Who did it? *We must know!*' He stiffened as one of the man's blackened hands reached out to seize his lapel. 'You are dying. Do this thing before it is too late.'

The man's head lolled, and Bolitho could almost feel the release from pain as death crept over him.

'Vyvyan.' For a brief instant some strength rebelled, and with it came another agony. Blount screamed the name, '*Vyvyan!*'

Hugh Bolitho stood up and removed his hat. As if to allow the rain to wash away what he had seen.

Robins whispered, 'That last shout done for him, sir.'

Hugh Bolitho heard him and turned away from the corpse. 'For more than one man.'

As he brushed past, Bolitho saw the claw-like stain on his white lapel, left there by the dying man. In the flickering light it looked like the mark of Satan.

'On the Uproll!'

Bolitho and Dancer trained their telescopes on the jetty and watched the sudden activity amongst the jolly boat's crew which had been waiting there for over an hour.

'We shall soon know, Dick.' Dancer sounded anxious.

Bolitho lowered the telescope and wiped his face free of rain. He was soaking wet, but like Dancer and most of the *Avenger*'s company had been unable to relax, to be patient while he awaited his brother's return.

That first horror of finding the man who had been left to die, the excitement of knowing Dancer had been right about Vyvyan's implications, had already gone sour. Colonel de Crespigny himself and a troop of dragoons had ridden hard to Vyvyan Manor, only to be told that Sir Henry had left on an important mission, and no, they did not know where, or when he might return. Sensing the colonel's uncertainty, the steward had added coldly that Sir Henry was unused to having his movements queried by the military.

So there was no evidence after all. Apart from that last, desperate accusation of a dying man, they had nothing. No stolen cargo, no muskets, brandy or anything else. There were plenty of signs that people had been there. Hoof-marks, wheel-tracks and traces of casks and loads being hauled about in a great hurry. But what remained would soon be washed away in the continuous downpour. In any case it was not evidence.

Dancer said quietly, 'It will be Christmas Day tomorrow, Dick. It may not be a happy one.'

Bolitho looked at him warmly. Dancer was the one who would be spared all enquiry but the briefest statement. His position, to say nothing of his father's importance in the City of London, would see to that. And yet he felt just as vulnerable as the Bolitho family which had got him involved in the first place.

The boatswain's mate of the watch called, 'Cap'n's boat 'as just shoved off, sir!'

'Very well. Call the side party. Stand by to receive him.'

It might well be the last time Hugh Bolitho was received aboard in command, here or anywhere else, he thought. Hugh Bolitho clambered over the side and touched his hat to the side party.

'Call the hands and hoist the boats inboard.' He squinted up at the flapping masthead pendant. 'We will get under way within the hour.' He looked at the midshipmen for the first time and added bitterly, 'I'll be glad to be rid of this place, home or not!'

Bolitho tensed. So there was no last minute hope, no reprieve.

As Dancer and the boatswain's mate hurried forward, Hugh Bolitho said in a calmer tone, 'I am required to make passage to Plymouth forthwith. The members of my company I put aboard a prize are assembled there, so your appointment as my senior will no longer be needed.'

'Did you hear anything about Sir Henry Vyvyan?'

He saw his brother give a shrug as he answered, 'De Crespigny was duped like the rest of us. You remember that bullion which the dragoons were suddenly and mysteriously required to escort at Bodmin? Well, we have now learned that it was Vyvyan's property. So while the revenue men and our people were being set upon by his ruffians, and cut to pieces, Vyvyan's booty was coolly being put aboard a vessel at Looe, after being escorted by the very soldiers who have since been searching for him!' He turned and looked at him, his face strained and seemingly older. 'So as he slips away to France, probably to negotiate for more weapons for his private wars, I will have to face the consequences. I thought I could run before I could walk. But I was outwitted, and beaten without knowing it!'

'And Sir Henry is *known* to be aboard this vessel?' He could picture the man even as he spoke.

It would be a triumph for Vyvyan, who had led a dangerous but rewarding life before coming to Cornwall. And when it had all quietened down he would come back. It was unlikely he would be challenged by the authorities again.

Hugh Bolitho nodded. 'Aye. The vessel is the *Virago*, a new and handy ketch-rigged sloop. Vyvyan has apparently owned her for a year or so.' He swung away, the rain pouring unheeded down his features. 'She might be anywhere by now. My orders from the port admiral *suggest* that a King's ship may be required to investigate, but nothing more than that.' He slapped his hands together, despairing, final. 'But *Virago* is fast, and will outsail anything in this weather.'

Gloag came clumping on deck, his jaw working on some salt beef.

'Sir?'

'We are getting under way, Mr Gloag. Plymouth.'

No wonder Hugh wished to be rid of the place. Danger from an enemy, or across the marks of a duelling pitch he could take with ease. Scorn and contempt he could not.

Bolitho watched the dripping boats being swayed inboard, the seamen's bodies shining like metal in the heavy rain.

To Plymouth, and a court of enquiry. It was not much of a way to end a year.

He thought of the nearness of success, the callous way Vyvyan had directed the deaths and the plunder of wrecked ships. He thought too of Dancer's face as the troopers had aided him into the house, the livid bruises on his shoulders. How his captors had threatened to put out his eyes. All the time they had been on the fringe of things. Now it was over, and they were as much in the dark as ever.

His brother said, 'I'm going below. Inform me when the anchor is hove short.'

a foolish gesture after all, a last desperate attempt to settle the score. They had sighted nothing, not even an over-zealous fisherman. Which was hardly surprising on this of all days, Bolitho thought bitterly.

He squinted through the rain, his stomach queasy as it rebelled against the liberal ration of rum which had been sent round the vessel. Trimming sails, reeling from one tack to another, left little chance for lighting the galley fire and getting something hot for all hands. Bolitho had decided he would never drink rum again if he could help it.

Gloag had been right about the weather too, as he always seemed to be. The rain was still falling steadily, cutting the face and hands like icy needles. But it had lessened in strength, and with the slight easing had come a strange mist which had joined sea to sky in one blurred grey curtain.

Bolitho thought of his mother, picturing the preparations for the Christmas fare. The usual visitors from surrounding farms and estates. Vyvyan's absence would be noticed. They would all be watching Harriet Bolitho, wondering, questioning.

He stiffened as he heard his brother coming on deck again. He had barely been absent for more than one half-hour at a time since leaving Falmouth.

Bolitho touched his salt-stained hat. 'Wind's holding steady, sir. Still southerly.'

It had backed during the night and was pounding into the *Avenger*'s great mainsail from almost hard abeam, thrusting her over until the lee scuppers were awash.

Gloag's untidy shape detached itself from the

opposite side and muttered, 'If it rises again or veers
sir, we'll 'ave to be thinkin' about changin' tack.' He
pouted doubtfully, unwilling to add to his commander's worries, but knowing his responsibility was
for them all.

Bolitho watched the uncertainty and the stubborn-
ness fighting one another on his brother's wind-
reddened face. The cutter was about ten miles due
south of the feared Lizard, and as Gloag had said,
with a rising gale they could find themselves on a
lee shore when they eventually went about, if they
did not take care.

Hugh Bolitho crossed to the weather side and
stared fixedly into the stinging rain.

Partly to himself he said, 'Damn them. They've
done for me this time.'

The deck lifted and slithered away again, men
falling in sodden bundles, cursing despite fierce looks
from their petty officers. Soon now. They were late
already in responding to the admiral's summons. If
Hugh Bolitho delayed much longer the wind might
decide to play a last cruel trick on him and shift
direction altogether.

He looked at his younger brother and gave a bleak
smile. 'You are thinking too hard again, Richard. It
shows.'

Bolitho tried to shrug it off. 'It was my suggestion
to make this search. I merely thought. . . .'

'Don't blame yourself. It is almost over. On the
noon bell we'll bring her about. And it *was* a good
idea of yours. Any other day the channel would be
dense with shipping and it would have been like a

needle in a haystack. But Christmas Day?' He sighed.
If the fates had been kinder, and we could *see*, who
knows?'

He added, 'We had better see to our extra canvas,
in case the weather worsens presently.' It was his
duty to attend to the vessel's needs, but his voice
showed that his thoughts were elsewhere, still seeking
his enemy. 'Get aloft to the yard and check the stuns'l
booms, and tell Mr Pyke we'll need to take in a reef
shortly.' He peered up at the wind-hardened topsail,
the angry jerking of shrouds and braces as his command met the challenge of sea and tiller.

Dancer had also come on deck, looking pale and
dishevelled.

'I'll go, sir.'

Hugh Bolitho gave a tired smile. 'Still no head for
heights, Richard?'

The brothers looked at each other, and Dancer,
who knew only one of them, could sense they were
closer than they had been for a long time.

As Dancer clambered into the weather shrouds,
Bolitho said, 'I'm glad you asked me to join *Avenger*.'
He looked away, embarrassed that it was so hard to
speak like this.

Hugh Bolitho nodded slowly. 'Aboard the old
Gorgon I expect they're envying you at ease beside a
full table. If they only knew. . . .'

He looked up, showing his anxiety, as Dancer
yelled, 'Deck there! Sail on the weather bow.'

Even as his cry faded, eight bells chimed out from
the forecastle. They had been following the other
vessel all this time without being able to see her. She

could only be the *Virago*. Had to be. Another fe
minutes and *Avenger* would have come about, allo
ing her prey to slip away once and for all.

Pyke and Truscott, the gunner, came hurrying af
their hair ragged with spray, their bodies so steep
angled to the deck they looked like drunken sailo
with three sheets to the wind.

Pyke shouted, 'I'll go aloft to be sure, sir!' H
teeth were bared, as if this was too personal to l
shared.

Hugh Bolitho handed his hat to a seaman an
snapped, 'No. I will go myself.'

They all watched in silence. If Dancer had n
gone aloft they would have sailed to Plymouth i
ignorance. Hugh Bolitho, his coat tails flappir
around his white breeches like twin pendants, pause
merely briefly beside the midshipman before cor
tinuing up and further still until his shape w
blurred in mist and rain. When he reached the to
sail yard he stopped, and with his arms wrappe
around the madly vibrating mast peered ahead.

In two minutes he returned to the deck, his fac
expressionless as he said, 'She's *Virago*. No doubt abo
it. Two masts, ketch-rigged, carrying a lot of canva
Only his eyes were alive, bright like little fires as l
thought it out. 'She has the wind-gage of course, b
no matter.' He took a few paces to the compass ar
then eyed each sail in turn. 'Set the jib, Mr Pyke, ar
then send the hands aloft and run out the boon
from the yard. With stuns'ls she'll even outpace th
sloop.' His eyes flashed as he added sharply, 'C
someone will answer to me!'

Dancer was called down to the deck, and an experienced seaman sent aloft to take his place. As he arrived, breathless and soaked in rain and spray, he exclaimed, 'A change of luck, sir!'

Hugh Bolitho tightened his jaw. 'We need skill today, Mr Dancer, but I'll grant you I'll not send any luck away!'

Straining and pitching, her sails booming under the pressure, *Avenger* responded to their combined efforts. Like huge ears, the studding sails were run out on either beam, so that with the yards braced round she presented a tremendous pyramid of canvas before the wind.

It was a strange sensation, and sometimes frightening, Bolitho thought, as the cutter battered her way through crests and troughs alike, the spray bursting over the weather bulwark in solid sheets. There was still no sign of the *Virago*, and from what Dancer had described, there was little to see, even from the yards. Her hull was lost in sea mist, while like disembodied ins her sails towered above it, an easy task for the keen-eyed lookout.

Bolitho thought it unlikely that Vyvyan's sailing master was bothered at the possibility of a sea chase. Not at this stage. Vyvyan probably knew more about local ship movements even than the Admiralty, and would imagine *Avenger* snug in harbour, or tail between legs on her way back to face the admiral's wrath.

They were probably celebrating, somewhere up ahead. Christmas, victory over the King's authority, and a booty Bolitho could not even begin to imagine.

And why not? Vyvyan had won all the tricks. And now he was safely around the Lizard and would be well clear of the Scillies when he eventually broke into the vast desert of the Atlantic.

He heard Truscott ask, 'What pieces will she be carryin', sir?'

Hugh Bolitho sounded preoccupied as he scanned the sails again, searching for some possible danger or weakness.

'Much as ourselves normally. My guess is that Sir Henry Vyvyan will have a few extra surprises however, so be vigilant, Mr Truscott. I want no haphazard shooting today.' His tone hardened. 'This is not a mere fight. It is a matter of honour.'

Bolitho heard him. He sounded as if it was another duel. Something to be settled in the only way he knew. Perhaps this time, he was right.

Gloag called, 'Rain's movin' off, sir!'

It was hard to tell the difference, Bolitho thought. There was more spray coming inboard than rain, and the pumps were going busily all the time, so that he guessed a good portion of sea-water had found its way below.

There was a different light, not anything like the sun, and yet the tossing wave crests were brighter, their deep troughs less grey.

The helmsman cried, 'Steady she goes, sir! West sou'-west!'

Bolitho held his breath. Incredible. In spite of the powerful wind, Gloag had brought her three full points into it, with every sail and spar cracking and booming like a miniature battle.

Hugh Bolitho saw his expression and gave a quick
od. 'I told you, Richard. She handles well!'

A yell from the lookout put an end to speculation.
Deck there! Ship on the lee bow!'

Peploe, the sailmaker, bustling past with his mates
prepare for the first exploding piece of canvas,
oked at the acting-master and grinned. 'Got 'im!
Ve'm to wind'rd of th' bugger now!'

The lookout shouted, 'She's sighted us!'

They stared, fascinated, as the other vessel seemed
expand out of the receding rain like a spectre. She
as moving well, the sea creaming back from her
re-foot in an unbroken white moustache.

Someone gasped as smoke belched from her quar-
r, and before the smoke had been thrust aside a
all slammed through *Avenger*'s sails and rigging,
pping holes in the starboard studding sail and main
ike.

'By God, the old fox is still alert!' Hugh Bolitho
rned to watch the ball pounding across the waves.
le strode to the lee side and trained his telescope on
is adversary. 'Load and run out, if you please. I see
need for a challenge. That has already been offer-
!' He left the *Avenger*'s small broadside to Truscott
id said in a quieter tone, 'That was a powerful
iece. A nine-pounder at least. Probably put aboard
ith this in mind.'

Another bang, and a ball whimpered past the taff-
il before throwing up a waterspout well off the lar-
ard quarter.

Hugh Bolitho said angrily, 'Run up the colours.'

He watched as the gunner signalled from the fore-

deck that the guns were all loaded and run out. Wit
the hull at such an angle it had been easy to thrust th
six-pounders tightly against their ports, but less eas
to fire with any accuracy. The sea was barely inche
below each port, and the crews drenched with eac
savage plunge.

'On the uproll!'

Five tarred hands were raised along the bulwark
five slow-matches poised, hissing, above each touc
hole.

Then, *'Fire!'*

The sharp explosions were closely joined, jarrin
the deck, probing the ears, as shouting and cheerin
the crews hauled in their guns to swab out and reloa
with a minimum of delay.

Above the swaying hull men swarmed like monkey
to repair severed cordage, to take in the studdin
sail, which because of the wind's strength had tor
itself to shreds. And it had taken only one shot to d
it.

Crash.

The cutter shook violently, and Bolitho knew tha
a ball had at last hit the hull, and possibly close t
the water-line.

Bolitho steadied a glass on the other vessel. In
stantly her masts and yards sprang alive in the len
and he saw tiny figures moving around the deck, o
working at braces and halliards like the *Avenger*'s men

He winced as the next puny broadside banged ou
from the starboard battery. He saw the balls splash
ing around the *Virago*'s handsome counter, or fallin
well astern of her. The guns would not bear, but t

give the crews a chance Hugh would have to sail even closer to the wind, and so lose time and lengthen the range. He saw a brief, stabbing flash from the other vessel's quarter, imagined he saw a black blur before the iron ball ripped through the bulwark and tore along the deck like a saw. Men yelled and ducked, but one of the helmsmen was almost cut in half before the ball smashed its way through the opposite side.

Voices bellowed orders, feet slithered in spray and blood as more men ran to tend the wounded, to take control of the tiller.

Virago was drawing away now, and as Bolitho moved his glass still further he saw a patch of green on her poop and guessed it was Vyvyan in the long coat he often wore for riding.

Gloag shouted, "S'no use, sir! Much more o' this an' we'll lose every spar!'

As he spoke another ball hissed through the shrouds and brought down the other studding sail complete with boom, cordage and a trailing tangle of canvas. Men dashed with axes to hack it free, as like a sea-anchor it floundered alongside, hampering their progress.

Hugh Bolitho had drawn his sword. He said calmly, 'Make this signal, Mr Dancer. *Enemy in sight.*'

Dancer, used to the instant discipline of a ship of the line, was running to the halliards with his signal party before he properly understood. There was nobody to signal to, but Vyvyan might not realize it.

Even as the signal jerked up to the yard and broke to the wind *Virago*'s master would be advising

Vyvyan to change tack, to beat further south fo
fear of being caught in a trap and driven into Moun
Bay by two instead of one pursuer.

'It's working!' Dancer stared at Bolitho wit
amazement.

The *Virago*'s sails were in disarray as she edge
closer to the wind, her yards braced so tightly roun
they were almost fore and aft. But more flashes spa
from her side, and several lengths of rigging an
some shattered blocks joined the litter on *Avenger*
deck.

A great crash shook the hull, and a chorus of shout
and yells made the seamen scatter as the topmas
with yards and flailing stays plunged down, splinter
ing yet again above the guns before lurching ove
the side.

Hugh Bolitho waved his sword. 'Put the helm
down, Mr Gloag! We will steer as close as we can!
As the tiller went over and the great mainsail swung
on its boom, obedient to the straining seamen, h
added for Truscott's benefit, *'Now! On the uproll!'*

With the range falling away, and fully conscious o
their own peril, each gun captain fired at will.

Bolitho gritted his teeth and tried to ignore th
terrible cries from the wounded men below the mast
He concentrated every fibre as he watched for th
fall of *Avenger*'s ragged broadside.

Then he heard the crack. Across the angry wav
crests and above the din of battle he heard it, and
knew one of the six-pounders had found its mark.

And it only needed one. Under full sail, standing
dangerously into the wind to beat away fron

venger's invisible ally, the sloop seemed to quiver, as
striking a sand-bar. Then, slowly at first, then with
errifying speed, the complete array of canvas began
o stagger aft. The topgallant mast, the fore-topmast
nd yards, driven with all the speed of wind and strain,
ollapsed along the deck, changing the *Virago* from a
horoughbred to a shambles in seconds.

Hugh Bolitho snatched up a speaking trumpet,
is eyes never leaving the other vessel as he
houted, 'Stand by to shorten sail! Mr Pyke, prepare
o board!'

Then there was a new sound, rumbling and spread-
ng as if from the *Avenger* herself. But it was her com-
any whose voices mingled in something like a growl,
s snatching up their weapons they ran to their
ations for boarding.

Dancer said, 'There'll be more of them than us,
r!'

Hugh Bolitho pointed his sword and looked along
he blade as if sighting a pistol.

'They'll not fight.'

He watched the range falling away, the sloop
reading out on either bow as if to snare them.

'Now, Mr Gloag.'

The sails were already being taken in, and as the
ller went over again the *Avenger*'s bowsprit came up
nd into the wind, while between the two hulls the
a was lost in their shadows.

The tiny figures on the *Virago*'s deck had become
en, and the faces had sharpened into individuals,
me of whom Bolitho recognized, a few he had even
en in Falmouth.

Hugh Bolitho stood at the bulwark, his voice shar[p] through the trumpet.

'Surrender! In the King's name!' His sword swun[g] like a pointer towards the levelled swivel guns. 'O[r] we fire!'

With a lurch the two vessels came together, bring[-] ing down more broken rigging and spars to add t[o] the confusion. But despite a few defiant shouts not [a] shot was fired, not a sword was raised.

Hugh Bolitho walked slowly between his me[n] towards the place where he would board. Taking h[is] time, looking for some last spark of defiance.

Bolitho followed him with Dancer, hangers draw[n] conscious of the oppressive silence which had eve[n] quietened the wounded.

These were not disciplined sailors. They had n[o] flag, no cause to guide or inspire them. At th[is] moment of truth they knew they would not escape, s[o] that personal safety had become all important. T[o] lay evidence against a man they had once called friend, to face prison rather than a gibbet. Som[e] would even now be hoping to be freed altogether b[y] using lies with no less skill than their cruelty.

Bolitho stood at his brother's shoulder on the *Vi[r]- ago*'s deck, watching the cowed faces, feeling the[ir] fury giving way to fear, like the blood that had fade[d] away in the blown spray.

Sir Henry Vyvyan would probably be able t[o] plead for some special privilege even now, he though[t] But Hugh's victory was complete all the same. Th[e] ship, her cargo and enough prisoners to make Moun[t] Bay safe for years to come.

'Where is Sir Henry?'

A small man in a gilt-buttoned coat, obviously the sloop's master, pushed towards them, his forehead badly cut by flying wood splinters.

'Worn't my fault, sir!'

He reached out to touch Hugh Bolitho's arm but the sword darted between them like a watchful snake.

So he backed away, while Bolitho and the others followed him towards the poop, which had taken the full brunt of the falling mast.

Sir Henry Vyvyan was pinned underneath one massive spar, his face screwed into a mask of agony. But he was still breathing, and as the sailors stood over him he opened his one eye and said thickly, 'Too late, Hugh. You'll not have the pleasure of seein' me dance on a rope.'

Hugh Bolitho lowered his sword for the first time, so that its tip rested on the deck within inches of Vyvyan's cheek.

He replied quietly, 'I had intended a more fitting end for you, Sir Henry.'

Vyvyan's eye moved towards the glittering blade and he said, 'I would have preferred it.'

Then with a great groan he died.

The sword vanished into its scabbard, the movement final, convincing.

'Cut this wreckage away.' Hugh Bolitho sounded almost untouched by the events and the sights around him. 'Pass the word to Mr Gloag. We will require a tow until a jury-rig can be arranged.'

Only then did he look at his brother and Dancer.

'That was well done.' He glanced at the flag which was being run up to the *Virago*'s peak, the same one which, although torn ragged by wind and gunfire, still flew above his own command. 'The best Christmas gift I have ever been given!'

Dancer grinned. 'And maybe there will still be something left at Falmouth to celebrate with, eh Dick?'

As they made their way back to their own vessel, Bolitho paused and looked aft towards the great heap of wreckage.

His brother was still standing beside the trapped body in the long green coat.

Perhaps, even now, he was thinking that Sir Henry Vyvyan had beaten him?